TWO GIRLS.
ONE HORSE.
A PROMISE.

COTEAU
BOOKS

www.coteaubooks.com

TWO GIRLS.
ONE HORSE.
A PROMISE.

TAKING
THE
REINS

Dayle Campbell Gaetz

Edited by Alison Acheson
Designed by Scott Hunter
Typeset by Susan Buck
Printed and bound in Canada at Imprimerie Gauvin

FSC
www.fsc.org
RECYCLED
Paper made from
recycled material
FSC® C100212

Library and Archives Canada Cataloguing in Publication

Gaetz, Dayle, 1947-
    Taking the reins / Dayle Campbell Gaetz.
Issued also in electronic formats.
ISBN 978-1-55050-552-8
    I. Title.
PS8563.A25317T34 2013   jC813'.54   C2013-900080-1

Gaetz, Dayle, 1947-
    Taking the reins [electronic resource] / Dayle Campbell Gaetz.
Electronic monograph.
Issued also in print format.
ISBN 978-1-55050-553-5 (PDF).--ISBN 978-1-55050-740-9 (EPUB).--
ISBN 978-1-55050-741-6 (MOBI)
    I. Title.
PS8563.A25317T34 2013   jC813'.54   C2013-900081-X

Library of Congress Control Number 2012954421

COTEAU
BOOKS

2517 Victoria Avenue
Regina, Saskatchewan
Canada   V6V 1N2
www.coteaubooks.com

10 9 8 7 6 5 4 3 2 1

Available in Canada from:
Publishers Group Canada
2440 Viking Way
Richmond, British Columbia

Available in the US from:
Orca Book Publishers
www.orcabook.com
1-800-210-5277

Coteau Books gratefully acknowledges the financial support of its publishing program by: The Saskatchewan Arts Board, including the Creative Industry Growth and Sustainability Program of the Government of Saskatchewan via the Ministry of Parks, Culture and Sport; the Canada Council for the Arts; the Government of Canada through the Canada Book Fund; and the City of Regina Arts Commission.

To all the girls and women,
both foreign and native born, who helped
tame these "wild and free" colonies.

Katherine

A Lady in Breeches – On Sunday last, a...lady was observed on Esquimalt wharf, about the time of the departure of the *Oregon*, wearing a complete suit of gentleman's clothes – breeches and all! After the steamer had cast off, she quietly mounted a fine horse, in true gentlemanly style – which means with a pedal extremity on either side of the animal – and rode off briskly towards Victoria, leaving a large and curious crowd of spectators to wonder as to who she was, whence she came, and whither she was bound...

– *The British Colonist*, April 15, 1862

TWO GIRLS. ONE HORSE.

1

The saddle creaked as Katherine leaned forward to run her fingers through the thick hair of Nugget's mane. "Good girl," she whispered, "only this last rough bit and we're almost home." She loosened the reins and let Nugget pick her own way down a narrow, rock-strewn trail carved into the side of a steep rock face. Below them the Fraser River slid seaward, filling the valley with its cavernous roar.

Her horse flinched when Duke snorted, so close at Katherine's heels she felt his warm, moist breath clean through the fabric of George's old breeches. "You're doing fine," she reassured Nugget. She would trust her life with this horse. Not so much with her brother.

Katherine glared over her shoulder at him. "What are you trying to do? Knock us over the edge?"

George squirmed in the saddle. He pushed his wide-brimmed hat further back on his forehead and urged Duke even closer, trying to squeeze past Katherine in spite of the risk. "Must you be so slow?"

"What's your great hurry, George? Not so long ago you couldn't wait to run away from the farm. Now you'd endanger both our lives simply to arrive home a few minutes faster?"

He kept his eyes on the trail ahead. "I wouldn't expect you to understand, your being such a young girl and all."

"Understand what?" she snapped. Honestly, sometimes talking to her brother was like chatting with a fence post.

His eyes remained on the trail as if Katherine weren't there at all. "A man needs some danger in his life. Trudging behind you bores me."

"Oh! Then if risking your own life is so important, you can go right ahead, but you have no right to endanger the horses or me either."

George's gaze skimmed past her and slid over the cliff edge to the fast-moving water at its base. His head and shoulders dipped. His hat slipped low on his forehead. He grunted and eased Duke a safe distance behind Nugget.

Katherine returned her attention to Nugget. "You may not have noticed, girl, but I think George just apologized to us."

Before long the trail leveled off and widened into a dusty road between dry grasses. George didn't waste a second. He moved up beside Nugget, pushed his hat back, and urged Duke into a gallop. Leaning low over the white horse's outstretched neck, George flung a challenge over his shoulder. "You'll never catch us now!"

"No, and I don't want to either!" Katherine shouted, but knew he couldn't hear. Horse and rider vanished in a swirl of dust until all she could see of them was the ghost-white shape of Duke's rump and the occasional glint of a horseshoe rising and falling like a silver-toothed grin, mocking her through rising clouds of dust.

Katherine had no reason to hurry, no reason to race her brother today. Not like before. The day she caught up with George's pack-train and told him he was needed at home, he had refused to listen. He told her to go home where she belonged. He called her ridiculous and said she could never keep up with him because she was a girl. Not that his horse was faster or he a more experienced rider. Only that she was a girl.

Katherine had felt a flash of anger but quashed it in favor of tossing out a challenge. "Not only can I keep up to you, I can beat you. And what's more, I'll bet on it. If I lose, I'll go home, empty-handed, without another word. If I win, you'll come with me and you won't complain, not once."

How George had laughed at that, so sure of himself. So sure he would win. What man couldn't beat his little sister in a horse race?

Katherine patted Nugget's neck, just ahead of the saddle horn. "We showed those two, didn't we, girl?" She chuckled, remembering the shock on her brother's face when she sped past him on her beautiful bay mare. "You're the best horse ever."

And now they were almost home.

Katherine didn't want this adventure to end. Not yet. She had never known such freedom as she experienced over these past days, nor half so much excitement. She would like nothing better than to turn around and run away from her lonely life on this wretched farm where everything she did reminded her of Susan.

She blinked back tears. It seemed like years since her sister had died. Years since their journey from England came to such a tragic end. Since that ghastly day nothing had gone right until at last George could take no more and ran off in search of gold.

Would her parents ever forgive her for chasing after him? Running off after leaving only the briefest of notes on her pillow?

Dear Mother and Father,

Don't worry about me. There is something I must do. I will be back in a few days.

Love, Katherine

She had dressed in George's old clothes, tucked the gold rose nugget in her pocket, safely wrapped in a small cloth bag for fear of losing it. Then she tiptoed from the cabin, carrying her boots. Guided by silvery moonlight she set off on foot to find her brother, whose help was needed at home since Father's injury.

Now Katherine touched the small hard lump in her pocket. Susan's gold rose nugget protected her and kept her sister close. Without it, Katherine would never have gotten Nugget, and without such a fine horse she would never have caught up to her brother.

As if sensing her mood, Nugget came to a full stop. "Thank you, girl." She patted the warm softness of Nugget's neck. "I'll be all right now."

Nugget plodded to the top of a small rise and stopped again. Nestled beneath tall firs, the cabin waited for Katherine, looking even smaller than she remembered. Dust settled on the trail behind her brother as he galloped ahead, reined Duke in, and leaped from the saddle. Before his feet hit the ground, the cabin door burst open and Mother came flying out. The wide skirt of her long, blue dress billowed around her as she darted across the porch, down the two steps, and reached up to throw her arms around her son.

Katherine stared. Mother was always so prim and proper, so unwilling, or unable, to show affection. But there she stood, hugging George so hard his eyeballs must be popping clear out of their sockets. She felt a quick tightness in her chest. Where was Father? Why didn't he come out of the cabin? Is that why Mother was so emotional? Had Father's condition worsened?

George escaped from their mother's embrace and hurried into the cabin. Katherine's fingers twisted around Nugget's reins. She swallowed. Moments later, two figures emerged through the rustic wooden door. George's arm encircled a smaller man, helping him onto the porch. Surely that could not be...

The thin, hunched-over man raised his hand to shield his eyes from the sun and peer in her direction. Then he waved one arm above his head as if he might be glad to see her. Katherine shook her head. She knew her father, and he would never show half so much excitement. How could this be?

Mother lifted her long skirt in both hands and began running toward Katherine. In the next second, Katherine couldn't wait to be home. She tapped her heels against Nugget's sides and the horse broke into a canter.

They were twenty feet apart when Mother stopped abruptly. Her hand flew to her mouth. Katherine pulled so hard on the reins Nugget reared up and dropped to a standstill. Her mother stumbled backward, raising her arm as if to push Katherine away.

What was wrong?

Mother glanced over her shoulder at George, then back again to Katherine, both hands pressed over her mouth. Her soft blue eyes travelled from Katherine's left boot snug in the stirrup, up and over Katherine's leg clad in George's old breeches, filthy from so many days on the trail through dust and rain and nights sleeping on the ground. Her gaze continued past the grimy shirt and vest to Katherine's face, shadowed by a wide-brimmed hat.

Katherine had become so used to dressing like a boy she had forgotten how very different she must look. Even her own mother didn't recognize her. Katherine smiled. "It's me, Mother. It's Katherine."

Mother's face hardened. Katherine bit her lip and stared down at her hands, twisting at the brown leather reins. Why had she ever thought her parents might understand, that they might even be grateful to her? She made a half-hearted attempt to explain. "I was afraid. I didn't want all those men out there to know I'm a girl because..."

"Katherine?" her mother interrupted. She ran to grab Nugget's bridle. "Get down from that horse this instant!"

Oh, Mother was so unfair! Katherine pressed her lips together and held her anger inside as she swung her right leg over the horse, slipped her left foot from the stirrup and dropped easily to the ground. She had tried so very hard to do the right thing but, as usual, had only managed to upset her mother by breaking some stupid rule. *Young ladies must always wear a long dress, never breeches. Young ladies must always ride side-saddle, never astride a horse.*

What would people think?

With the reins clutched tightly in her hand, Katherine

pressed close against the soft, reassuring warmth of Nugget's side and breathed in the strangely comforting scent of horse. She couldn't turn around and face her mother's anger. She simply could not.

"Katherine." Unexpectedly strong hands clasped her shoulders and swung her around.

Katherine stared at the hard line of her mother's lips, shut her eyes tight, and fought for composure. How could she make Mother understand? She opened her eyes. "Mother, I..." But her voice cracked, and she couldn't go on.

Mother's grasp slid to Katherine's upper arms. She studied her daughter's face as if she had never seen it before. "Katie? Oh, Katie, just look at you!" She reached up and whipped the hat off Katherine's head. "Your poor hair! You look exactly like a boy and I'm so..." Mother frowned. All traces of anger spilled out of her, suddenly, in the space of a breath. Her shoulders sagged and tears sprang into her eyes. "I'm so grateful to you."

Katherine couldn't believe what she heard. Grateful? Mother? To her?

Mother slipped an arm around her shoulders. "It was so clever of you to dress as a boy, Katie. With all those rough men arriving here from all parts of the world and so few women to remind them how to behave, a young girl cannot be too careful."

Katherine nodded, unable to speak.

"Come now, your father is waiting."

"Is he feeling better then?"

"Much. But he is unable to walk without help."

Katherine stood in front of her father. He looked so tired and frail leaning on George that she could scarcely comprehend he was the same man she had known all her life. The man who always got his own way, the angry man who frightened her with his harsh words and disapproving looks. Even more confusing were the tears that filled his chocolate-brown eyes.

"Kate," he whispered, and reached out to gently touch her cheek with his fingertips. "I was so afraid we would never see you again. We had no idea where you went."

"I'm sorry Father. I never meant to worry you, but I thought, with you being injured and all, we would need George to finish the well and barn and help get things ready for winter. I knew, if I asked, you would never let me go after him."

"Quite right." He pulled himself up a little taller, pushing away from George. "It is not fitting for a girl..."

"Peter! Not now," Mother interrupted.

Katherine stared at her parents, back and forth, one and the other. She wondered if there had been some huge mistake. Had she somehow stumbled into the wrong family? These people simply did not fit. Her mother never contradicted her father, not ever. If anyone in the family so much as disagreed with the tiniest thing he said, Father always got so angry his face turned purple and he spit out stupid, hurtful words that did not make any sense at all.

Katherine glanced at her brother. George stood absolutely still. His mouth gaped open and he eyed their parents as if he had no idea who they were. Then his eyes rolled to Katherine, his mouth snapped shut and he raised his eyebrows, up and down, up and down.

She grinned.

They both turned to Father who looked exhausted, as if the effort of getting angry was simply too much for him. He swayed on his feet, and Katherine took his arm to support him. "It's so good to be home!" she said, and meant it.

After dinner that evening, the family lingered around their hand-carved wooden table sipping sweet, hot tea. Dinner had been filling enough, if not terribly exciting. Fresh potatoes, carrots, and beans Katherine brought in from the garden. Cups of thick milk George managed to obtain from Genevieve, even though milking was not normally his chore. No bread, no butter, no meat.

"There has been so much to do with both of you gone," Mother explained. "Caring for your father, tending the garden, milking Genevieve, I haven't found a moment to bake bread or churn butter. And we are desperately short of supplies."

"Give me a list," George offered. "I'll ride into Hope tomorrow and Katherine can bake some bread."

"Oh, no." Katherine glared at her brother. "You're not doing that again, leaving me trapped on the farm while you go off and have fun in town. I'll take Nugget for supplies while you work on finishing the well you started before you ran off in some foolish search for gold."

"Katherine," he sneered, "I left for the Cariboo because our family needs money. And I'm not going to town for fun, only to get the things Mother needs."

Maybe. But if she let him get away with it now, everything would slip right back to the way it had been. She would be trapped on this farm for the rest of her life. "George, if you expect me to believe that..."

"Children!" Mother sat very straight, pressed her shoulders back, and frowned from George to Katherine, on opposite sides of the table.

"I am not a child," Katherine informed her. "I'm fourteen years old."

"And I most certainly am not a child," George said through clenched teeth.

Katherine scowled at her brother.

He dismissed her with a look, his blue eyes cold and hard. She stared down at her hands, clenched into tight fists on the table. Until this minute, she had dared hope they might get along better after spending so much time together on the trail, but it seemed George was determined to slip back into being his old, obnoxious self. "Oh," she said, "you think you're so marvelous just because you're nineteen? Well, let me tell you, George Harris, I can shoot a rifle better than you and beat you in a horseback race, and do a whole lot of other things better than you ever will. And what's more, you know it."

George grunted. He busied himself stirring cream into his tea.

"No one is going into town," Mother whispered.

Both George and Katherine turned to their father. He must be very ill to remain silent for so long. Indeed, Father's face had gone pale. His chin sank so low it threatened to dip into his plate of unfinished food. Father picked up his teacup but his hand shook so badly he replaced it, rattling, onto its saucer, slopping milky brown liquid over the rim. "It is not fitting for a young girl..."

"Ohhh! You keep saying that!" Katherine hissed. She refused to be told what was fitting and what was not. Why should she be bound by some silly rules made up in a country half the world away? Everything was different here. This land was huge and wild and free. She would not be a prisoner, confined to this one patch of land.

There was no answering anger from Father. Far from it. Instead of glowering at her, he seemed to shrink into himself. His chin sank even lower over his plate. Katherine closed her eyes, took a slow, deep breath, and let her anger fall away.

"Father," she said calmly, "I have travelled all the way up to the Thompson River with..." She stopped and took a quick sip of tea to cover her blunder. A shiver ran through her. She had almost said, *With William's help*, and only just caught herself in time. She must be more careful.

Katherine held her teacup with fingers daintily clasping the handle, exactly as Mother had taught her, and completed her sentence, "...without any problem. So I think I am capable of riding into Hope by myself."

"We could go together," George offered. "I'll take the wagon for supplies."

"Oh. Yes, of course," Katherine said, grateful for George's unexpected compromise.

Mother pushed her cup and saucer away. "Did no one hear me? No one is going into town." She placed both hands on the table, pushed herself heavily to her feet, and stumbled toward the open door.

Katherine and George stared across the table at each other. Again they both turned to Father, but he only gazed gloomily into his teacup as if unaware of all that was going on around him. Sister and brother stood and followed their mother outside.

They found her seated on the top step. Elbows resting

on her knees, she cupped her chin in both hands and gazed up at the mountain that loomed above their farm. Twilight shadows turned its topmost peak to gold and accentuated every crevice in the naked rock.

Katherine settled beside her mother. Something was troubling her. Something beyond the loss of Susan and the worry over Father. Katherine could see that now.

They stayed for a few minutes that way, sitting side by side, absolutely still, with George hovering behind them near the door. No one spoke until finally Katherine broke the silence. "Why don't you want us to go into town, Mother? Don't you trust us?" Another thought occurred to her. "Or are you ashamed of the way I look, with my short hair and sun-browned face?"

Mother's forehead sank to her knees, pressed against her two hands that rested there. "I only wish it were that simple," she whispered.

Katherine leaned closer. "Then what?"

"We have no money." Mother's voice was muffled by her full cotton skirt.

"What? None?"

"Very little," she said. "Barely enough for a sack of flour. What with the medicines I needed for your father, and the money he gave to George..." Her voice faded away.

After a moment, Mother spoke again, so quietly Katherine strained to hear. "I'm afraid your father has never been good with money. And of course our journey from England cost more than planned, due to our prolonged stay in San Francisco when..." Her voice collapsed altogether.

Katherine knew what Mother couldn't say. *When we all took ill, Susan worst of all.*

That night Katherine lay on her simple bed, so tired her entire body ached. She snuggled under the warm blanket and closed her eyes. She would sleep well.

No money.

Her eyes popped open.

They faced a long winter with not enough food and little money. Nothing to buy essential supplies. Fear crept into her belly. Katherine had never been poor, never been forced to go hungry, and the thought of it terrified her.

Would they have had enough if Father hadn't been hurt? Possibly. And that made it all her fault. If only she had called Father that morning, or paused to grab the gun herself, everything would be different. Instead she had raced from her bed waving her arms, furious at that mother bear and cub for digging up her precious vegetable garden. The cub had ambled away but its mother turned on Katherine, and when Father ran outside he was mauled trying to protect her.

If she had stopped to think, they might have dried bear meat in storage and a warm bearskin rug to help keep out winter's chill.

If it's your fault, then it's up to you to do something about it. The voice came out of the darkness, not Susan's voice exactly, but there nevertheless. It was a quiet voice that continued to give her direction whether she wanted it or not. Katherine tried to push it away but the idea caught hold. She had to make this right and there was only one way to do so.

Katherine stumbled out of bed and made her way through the dark to her bureau. She slid open the top drawer and felt inside until her fingers closed around the small cloth bag. She felt the hard lump inside and dropped it onto her hand. The gold rose nugget. Susan's final gift.

She climbed back into bed and curled on her side, clutching the nugget in her tightly closed fist. Sometimes she needed so badly to talk to her sister that it seemed impossible she could be gone forever. Tears trickled over her nose and onto her pillow. She had promised Susan to keep the golden rose for the rest of her life. How could she even think of selling it? She couldn't, she wouldn't. The nugget was all she had left of Susan, a token to keep her sister's memory alive for a lifetime.

And if they all died of starvation, is that what Susan would want? No, Susan would tell her to sell the nugget and purchase provisions.

Oh, but she had promised!

Katherine's thoughts kept going back and forth until at last she slipped into a troubled sleep.

She awoke with a start. Her room was black and close around her. She knew now that there was another choice, something else she could sell in place of the golden rose.

But how could she bear to part with Nugget?

2

Katherine rolled over, delighting in the soft ground beneath her body. Warm too – she had not felt so warm at night in a long time. But the fingers of her right hand ached. Why? And why were they clutched into such a tight fist?

She pulled her hand from beneath the blanket. Blinked away the fuzziness of sleep. Opened her eyes. Saw nothing but grey. But wait – directly in front of her was a square of warm light. A window.

Of course, that's why she felt so cozy. She was not curled beside a dead campfire with early morning dew making everything damp and chill, but snug in her own bed with a mattress and blankets to keep her warm. And yet her fingers ached. She opened them slowly to reveal the nugget. Pressed tight against her palm, it glowed deep gold. Katherine thought back to the first time she ever saw the nugget, held just this way in Susan's hand as they stood side by side on the steamer's deck.

"Do you see?" Her sister held the nugget, shimmering under a harsh southern sun. "It looks just like a rose, as if someone had carved it that way."

Katherine tucked the nugget back into its cloth bag but still held it in her hand. No. She could never sell the golden rose, not ever. How could she even think such a thing? Which left her no other choice. If she couldn't part with the gold nugget, she would need to sell its namesake.

Katherine was surprised how easily she came to accept this choice, once her decision was made. They did not need two horses on the farm, eating hay all winter long. With only Duke and Genevieve, there might be enough feed to last until spring. And the money from the sale would buy much-needed provisions.

As soon as her chores were done, she would ride into Hope and inquire if anyone was looking to purchase a strong, fast horse. She slid out of bed and picked up the little pile of clothing she had worn on her trip. Pants, shirt, vest and jacket all were filthy from long days on the trail. Come wash day she would scrub them clean, hang them in the sunshine to dry, then tuck them safely away. The possibility was still there, still hovering so close she could almost reach out and touch it. The possibility that one day she might wear them again.

She dressed in a cotton blouse and a full skirt that brushed the tops of her boots, then hurried outside. The first rays of sun peeked around the mountainside, landing on bright pearls of dew, making the fields sparkle like early frost. She wrapped her cold fingers around the milk pail handle. How long would it be until a real frost?

With the milking done, Katherine left the pail inside the shed and walked to the field where both horses were hobbled. Nugget raised her head and walked over to Katherine, uttering a soft snort. A snort that said so much. *Good Morning. I'm happy to see you. What shall we do today?*

Katherine reached up to rub her horse's broad forehead. Her eyes stung. "I'm so sorry..." she began, but couldn't go on. She turned away.

She walked to her garden, filled with an impossible hope that there might be more vegetables than she remembered. There were great holes in the long, neat rows she had worked so hard to cultivate all summer long. The bear had dug up potatoes, carrots and turnips, but not all were lost. Beet greens had been chomped down to nothing, but with luck there would still be beets beneath the soil. What remained needed to be dug up and stored for winter. If they were very careful, there might be enough to last until Christmas. She went back to retrieve the milk, her last hope gone.

Katherine announced her plans at the breakfast table. "I'm riding into Hope this morning," she said, "to see what I can get for my horse."

Mother replaced her teacup on its saucer and glanced up sharply. She opened her mouth as if to speak.

Katherine held her breath. Perhaps Mother had another suggestion? Some idea that had not occurred to her until this very moment?

But Mother only nodded and glanced toward Father, who spooned some porridge into his mouth, swallowed, and frowned. "You'd best leave that to George."

"No!" Katherine bit her lip to keep from saying more. Defiance was no way to handle her father, Katherine knew that now. She paused, took a quick breath, and made an effort to soften her voice. "Father, please. I bought Nugget myself, she's my horse and I'd like to be the one to sell her."

Katherine stopped, wondering if she should go on, but the words tumbled from her mouth before she could stop them. "Mother has a long list of supplies we need to see us through winter, and I know you won't want any of us to go without."

Mother's tongue clicked against the roof of her mouth. George gave his customary grunt. Katherine studied her father. Had she gone too far? Father felt guilty enough for bringing them here, to this wild, empty country where nothing turned out as he expected.

She would have been relieved that Father chose to sidestep her comment if he hadn't turned instead to inquiring about Nugget. "Katherine, I can't imagine how you purchased the horse in the first place. I was unaware that you had money of your own."

Oh. Oh no. Katherine had never told her family about Susan's gold nugget. It was a cherished secret, her private connection to Susan. But she couldn't lie to her father. She had no money of her own and he knew that well enough. "I had a gold nugget," she whispered, "that Susan gave me."

A hush fell over the room at the mention of her sister's name.

"And where did Susan get such a nugget?"

"From Mr. and Mrs. Roberts, aboard the steamer. They were returning from England to their plantation in Jamaica and Susan took care of their baby when all three were so awfully seasick. You see, they believed Susan saved Baby Rose's life and that's why they gave her the nugget. They thought it appropriate because it was shaped like a rose."

Should she mention the storekeeper in Yale? On the day Katherine went into his store to purchase supplies for her journey, she had offered the gold nugget as payment.

The storekeeper held it on his palm and turned it over with his fingertips.

"Where did you get this?" he demanded.

As it turned out, the storekeeper was Charles Roberts, the very man who had sent the nugget as a gift to his older brother's family when Baby Rose was born. "My brother wrote me of your sister," he said. "He is most grateful to her."

When Charles Roberts learned of Susan's death, he felt so sorry he refused to take any payment at all.

And so Katherine still had the nugget. Best to keep this information to herself, she decided. Yale was not so very far away, and if Father ever got talking to him, the storekeeper might reveal more than she wanted him to know. He might mention Katherine was not alone that day but had hired her friend, a young Indian guide named William, to help catch up to her brother.

"Susan took care of everyone," Mother broke into her thoughts. "Everyone except herself."

Father cleared his throat. "Nevertheless, it isn't fitting for a young girl..."

George slurped his last spoonful of hot porridge, drowned in fresh, warm milk, into his mouth and dropped his spoon, clattering into the empty bowl. "Seems to me," he began in his slow, clumsy way, "that Katherine rode the horse all the way up to Cariboo Country on her own. Seems to me, riding a few miles into Hope should not be a problem for her."

Katherine's mouth fell open. She pushed it shut with the heel of her hand. A grin threatened to spread across her face but she managed to suppress it.

"Well..." Father's face flushed pink, "...but she was

riding *astride* the horse, as if she were a..."

"Boy," George finished for him. "That was clever of her. Katherine never could have travelled so far dressed as a girl. And she would not have beaten me in a horse race by riding side-saddle, I can assure you."

"George is right, Peter," Mother said. "These colonies are teeming with men. From what I've heard, scarcely one in a hundred has a hope of finding a wife. Katherine was wise to disguise herself as a boy."

Katherine leaned closer to their father. "Is that what worries you, Father? That I will embarrass you by riding into town wearing breeches and using a man's saddle? Well, I won't, you see, because I'm wearing a skirt today."

Father glared from one of his children to the other and then at his wife. He rubbed a hand over the stubble on his chin. "I still don't like it," he muttered.

Katherine knew she had won. She could climb on Nugget this very morning and ride away from the farm. No one would object, not her father, not her mother, not even George. Well, especially not George. For the first time in years, George was on her side. She smiled, but somehow the smile didn't feel right. It stuck on her lips and wouldn't go any further. All her life Katherine had wanted to win an argument with her father, but now that it had happened, instead of feeling happy she felt hollow inside. "Maybe George could come with me," she offered – why, she wasn't at all sure, because she really wanted to go alone. But as soon as she said it, Katherine began to feel happier. Likely because her mother's shoulders relaxed, George leaned back, smiling, and her father sat up a little straighter.

Her fingers brushed against the deep pocket of her

skirt. She had not lied to her family, not exactly, even if she neglected to mention she still had Susan's gold nugget. She wondered if Susan would approve.

After breakfast Mother fetched a straw bonnet and placed it firmly on Katherine's head. The hat slid over her eyebrows and covered her ears. With fingers made strong over many months of kneading bread, milking Genevieve, and a dozen other tasks, Mother proceeded to tuck every last strand of Katherine's rich brown hair up under the hat.

"Ow!" Katherine complained. "You're hurting me."

Mother didn't ease up. "You mustn't let anyone see your hair like this. What on earth would they think?"

"That I have short hair?"

Mother's fingers worked even harder, hurting her with their fierce jabs. "Honestly, Katherine, sometimes you drive me to distraction!" Selecting a wide blue ribbon, she tied the hat on with a tight bow under Katherine's chin. Then she stepped back, planted her hands on her hips, and cocked her head to one side, frowning. "It will have to do."

Katherine picked up her mother's hand mirror. "I look ridiculous," she moaned. "I look like an enormous toadstool."

"If you don't want to go..."

"I do."

"Then you must promise me you will not remove the bonnet."

Reluctantly, Katherine agreed.

George hitched Duke to the wagon and Katherine followed behind on Nugget.

Almost as bad as the hat, she felt silly wearing a long

skirt after becoming used to the much more practical breeches. Worse even than the skirt or hat, however, was sitting on her horse side-saddle. She felt nervous having both legs on the same side, with her right leg bent at an uncomfortable angle. Katherine struggled to maintain her balance, fearing she would topple off at any second.

Nugget felt it too. The horse pressed her ears back and kept twisting her neck to look behind until Katherine patted her soft, warm neck. "It's all right, girl," she soothed. A lump rose in her throat. Nugget couldn't know this would be their last ride together.

They reached the dusty main street of Hope far too soon. A sternwheeler chugged around a bend in the Fraser, billowing black smoke as it readied itself to fight through the rapids up to Yale. Many of the sternwheelers bypassed Hope lately, since Governor Douglas decided to begin the Cariboo Wagon Road upriver at Yale.

Only two horses were in sight, one tied in front of the general store, the other hitched to a wagon farther down the road. Three men, each with a heavy beard, each wearing a wide-brimmed hat, jacket, vest, trousers and high boots, lounged on wooden chairs under the store's wide overhang. They drank coffee from tin mugs and discussed worldly matters.

As Katherine stopped her horse in front of the store she overheard one of the men say, "Biggest fish you can imagine. But it got away."

Another mumbled something about the biggest fish always getting away. Katherine smiled to herself, thinking of Father. He insisted that men only conversed on important topics such as which side would win the civil war in the United States or whether British Columbia should remain a British colony or become an American state. Father said women wasted hours chattering incessantly about insignificant matters. That's why men must spend so much time sitting, talking, reading newspapers or simply staring into space. Who would solve the world's problems if they did not?

Katherine stopped listening. She had important matters of her own to consider. Such as how to dismount without making a fool of herself.

Her legs were set in an awkward position, both on Nugget's left side, her right knee bent around a curved pommel. How was she supposed to swing that leg over Nugget's back and slide to the ground as she had become used to doing? She managed to free her right leg and attempted to twist in the saddle in order to face toward the horse's left side. But her leg got tangled in the full fabric of her long skirt. Struggling to free it, she didn't notice her left boot slip out of the stirrup, so was surprised to find herself dangling from Nugget's side. She grabbed for the saddle horn. Too late, she remembered there wasn't one.

The men stopped talking. Katherine felt their eyes watching, imagined their amused expressions. Her cheeks burned. How could she get out of this gracefully? Over Nugget's back, she saw George leap from the wagon, loop Duke's reins over a wooden bar, and start over to help her.

Katherine hated feeling so clumsy. She hated those three men. Imagined them puffing on their pipes, leaning back in their chairs, enjoying her plight. She hated George too, for being so free while she hung here as helpless as a harpooned salmon. Well, she would not wait for her brother to save her. She would slip to the ground on her own with as much dignity as she could muster. Katherine grabbed the pommel and twisted her leg free of the skirt.

If only the heel of her right boot had not caught in the hem of her skirt, if only Nugget had not taken a quick step sideways, everything would have been fine. As it was, Katherine landed awkwardly on her left foot and lost her balance, toppling toward the horse just as Nugget took a second step away. Katherine collapsed onto the road. Her hands broke her fall, but her face landed in the dust.

"Katherine!" George crouched at her side. "Are you hurt?" He helped her to a sitting position.

Nothing hurt other than her pride. "No," she snapped, "I'm perfectly fine." But there was dust in her mouth and up her nose, she felt the gritty taste of it on her tongue, and she was sitting on the road while three men stared at her with their mouths gaping open as if they'd never seen anyone fall from a horse before.

"Your hat!" George jammed the bonnet back on her head.

She had not noticed until then that it was hanging down her back, the blue ribbon still tied at her throat. The men must have noticed, even though her brother was quick to block their view. Katherine could tell by the feel of it that the bonnet perched at a ridiculous angle on her head. She realized that her hair, so carefully tucked in by Mother, now hung loose beneath the brim. She glanced up at the men, at their wide eyes and half open mouths, and suddenly pictured exactly how she must look to them.

The laugh caught her by surprise. Her mouth twisted into a smile that spread across her face so fast it could not be subdued. Then a chuckle formed beneath her ribs, a chuckle that grew and expanded even as she bit hard on her bottom lip to hold it back.

Her eyes flicked to George. That was a mistake. Little creases pulled at the edges of his mouth and crinkled his eyes. Katherine was lost. She doubled over, gasping, chortling, helpless with laughter. In the next second they were all laughing, Katherine, George, and the three strangers, not one of them able to stop.

Finally George wiped his eyes and helped Katherine to her feet. She turned to the men and gave a graceful curtsey, which made them laugh even harder. One slapped his hand against his thigh. Another tried to speak but snorted with laughter instead. All three clapped to show their appreciation.

Sometimes it's difficult to make a laugh go away, especially if you haven't had a good chuckle in a long time. Katherine couldn't remember the last time she had laughed so hard. She tried to swallow the laughter, but it kept bubbling up and so she was grateful when George tied Nugget's reins for her. He took her arm, and the two of them hurried inside the store.

A woman of about Mother's age stood behind the counter. She had a thin, pretty face with clear, intelligent eyes. She smiled at the two laughing young people, her head cocked to one side as if hoping to share in the joke.

Katherine's laughter died. A memory threatened to overwhelm her. A memory of the last time she had laughed so helplessly and Mother had smiled in exactly the same way.

"Good Morning, Madame Landvoight," George greeted the storekeeper.

"Oh, so it is you, Georges!" She pronounced both "g"s in a soft, pretty way that made his name sound so completely different Katherine didn't recognize it at first. "You have returned so soon to town?"

George nodded. "My family needed me."

Madame Landvoight was a small and lively woman. When she turned her attention to Katherine, her eyes lingered for a moment on the large, crooked hat and the strands of short brown hair that hung down Katherine's neck and over her ears.

"And la jeune fille? She is your sister?"

"Uh, yes, my sister, Katherine." George paused. "Do you know, she rode halfway to the Cariboo after me? She cut her hair short and wore breeches so she would look like a boy."

Katherine glanced at George. For the second time today, he had spoken up for her. Might he actually be proud of her? She smiled at her brother, sorry for thinking she hated him.

"Eh, bravo, Katrine!"

Katherine turned back to Madame Landvoight. "Oh, but please, don't tell anyone else. You see, my parents don't approve of what I did."

"They will be proud of your ingenuity, yes? A pretty girl must be always careful!"

No one had ever called her pretty before. Her face was too long and narrow, her straight hair an ordinary, mousy brown, and her eyes too dark and too close together. Nothing like Susan's golden curls and bright blue eyes.

"And what may I help you wit' today, Katrine?"

Madame Landvoight had a musical way of speaking. Her voice rose at the end of every sentence as if she were asking a question, and the way she pronounced her words sounded quite exotic to Katherine. She especially liked the sound of own name. *Katrine.* But she had come here for a purpose and mustn't put it off any longer.

"We need supplies." Katherine glanced at her brother, who wandered away, his hands thrust into his pockets. She pulled a crumpled list from her pocket.

"C'est bon. You have come to the right place."

"The problem is..." Again Katherine glanced at George, but he had become quite fascinated by a shelf of canned goods. She drew a quick breath. "The problem is, we are a bit short of money. So..." Her voice broke. She stared straight ahead, over Madame Landvoight's left shoulder. "I want to sell my horse, Nugget. She's a beauty!"

Madame Landvoight frowned. "I am certain that you have a very good horse, Katrine. Sadly, I do not need a horse. I am so sorry."

Katherine stared down at the toes of her boots, coated thick with road dust. She pictured her face. It must be as dusty as the boots. She raised her hand to wipe it and the memory returned, slamming into her with such force she gasped with the pain of it.

She and Susan were at the hotel in Panama. They were exhausted, hot, and coated in a sticky layer of dust. Eager for a bath, Susan had poured some water into the huge tub. It was the colour of mud. She stared at the water, tears trickling down her dusty cheeks. She wiped at them but only succeeded in turning her entire face into a brown mask. Two weary blue eyes blinked out at Katherine. A huge mosquito landed on her sister's forehead. Without thinking, Katherine smacked it. Bright red blood mingled with the mud on Susan's face.

Katherine burst out laughing. Her sister looked puzzled until Katherine handed her a mirror. One glimpse of her reflection and Susan laughed as hysterically as Katherine. They laughed until their stomachs hurt and their mother walked in, head cocked to one side, wondering what could be so funny.

Now, this morning, only a few minutes ago, Katherine had laughed in that same way again. Her throat tightened, her eyes stung. How could she laugh with Susan lying in her grave?

Katherine's hand, clutching the list of supplies, fell to her side. She curled her fingers and crumpled it into a ball. George grunted. His heavy footsteps stomped out the door. It slammed shut behind him. Katherine turned to follow.

"There is one thing..." Madame Landvoight said.

Katherine stopped. "Yes?"

The storekeeper bent to retrieve a large book from under the counter. "There is a man who buys horses from all those poor miners who return from the Cariboo wit' nothing but rags to wear and their money all gone."

She opened the book. "Every autumn he takes the horses to Victoria, where men are eager to buy them. Some of those rich gentlemen will pay much money for a horse who will win races for them."

The storekeeper pronounced English words so differently from the way Katherine was used to hearing that she had to concentrate to understand.

"Nugget is very fast," she said, "and she loves to race."

"Ah, c'est bien."

"How can I find this horse trader?"

"Ah, there is the difficult part. He does not live here."

Katherine squeezed her eyes shut. If the horse trader didn't live in Hope, how could she find him and sell her horse to him? How could she get money for the supplies they needed right now?

"But wait, I have the idea." Madame Landvoight flipped through her book, muttering to herself. When she found the page she was looking for, she ran her finger down a column. "Ah, oui! You must talk wit' him in deux semaines...ah," she paused and pressed her fingertips to her forehead, "pardon, two weeks from tomorrow. He will visit our store on that day to deliver our winter supplies from Victoria."

Two more weeks. Today she would ride Nugget back home. She would ride Nugget every day for the next two weeks. Beyond that, she refused to think. "Thank you," she said. "I'll be here."

Madame Landvoight measured some flour into a sack and added it to a neat pile of packaged goods she had already placed on the counter. "For today, I have these things ready for you, Katrine," she said. She touched each package in turn. "Flour, sugar, tea, salt, bacon, and rolled oats for your porridge."

"But..." Katherine objected. How could she pay? Her parents would never accept charity. They would rather starve.

"You will pay me soon, when you have the money from the horse." Madame Landvoight handed a folded paper to Katherine. "I have written the amount for you."

"Oh, thank you so much." Katherine stuffed the paper into her pocket and scooped up all she could carry of the parcels. "You will never be sorry, I promise."

She hurried outside to find George.

3

Nugget pranced along the trail, head held high, sniffing the clean, crisp air and tugging at her reins. The horse wanted to run, but Katherine kept her reined in tight. The faster they travelled, the sooner they would arrive in Hope, and the distance wasn't nearly great enough as far as Katherine was concerned. Not today.

For the past two weeks she had spent every spare moment with Nugget. Together they had explored trails Katherine never knew existed. Every evening she had groomed the beautiful horse until her coat shone. And she told Nugget everything, just as she had once told Susan. Katherine knew her parents didn't understand this attachment she felt to a horse, but they did realize how much she was giving up and never once objected to her riding off on her own. She felt grateful for that.

Even today she had been able to get away on her own, thanks to George. He seemed to understand her need to be alone with Nugget on this final journey together. So when Father suggested George accompany her into Hope, George refused. "With so much work to do before winter sets in, I can't take the time. Katherine is perfectly capable of managing on her own and Madame Landvoight is expecting her, so there is no problem."

Katherine arrived in Hope to see most of the towns-folk gathered on the riverbank watching a sternwheeler pull into shore. She rode Nugget to a grassy area away from the crowd, where she dismounted and tied the reins loosely around the low branch of a young fir tree before starting back along the riverbank. The sternwheeler's bow nudged up against shore, ramps were placed against the bank, and men began to swarm ashore.

Standing slightly apart from the crowd, Madame Landvoight gazed down at the sternwheeler. Katherine started toward her. The storekeeper waved at someone below and Katherine turned to see. A man was walking up the ramp carrying a large parcel. There was something familiar about him...

Katherine backed away. Mr. Roberts! The storekeeper from Yale.

She scurried back to the far side of Nugget. "What is he doing here?" she demanded, leaning close against Nugget's side and absently rubbing her hand over the horse's powerful shoulder. "I may have been dressed as a boy when I met the man," she confided, "and introduced myself as 'Albert,' but I don't dare take the chance he'll recognize me."

She peeked over Nugget's back. "He just keeps on talking to Madame Landvoight. Why doesn't he go away? Doesn't he have something better to do with his time?"

Another man joined them. *That's him,* Katherine decided. *He must be the horse trader.* The three wandered over to a stack of goods that had been unloaded onto the grass. They talked for a few minutes longer before Mr. Roberts and Madame Landvoight left the other man and started toward her store.

"Finally." Katherine stepped out from behind Nugget.

Halfway to the store, Madame Landvoight stopped and glanced about as if looking for someone. She placed a hand over her eyes against the sun. Katherine slipped out of sight. After waiting for what seemed a long time, she peeked over Nugget's neck.

The two were walking toward her! But why? Did Mr. Roberts recognize the horse and want to take a closer look? Would he expect to take Nugget back now that her journey was completed?

"Katrine!" Madame Landvoight called.

It was too late to run away. Those two were almost upon her. How could she get out of this? Would Mr. Roberts recognize her? Perhaps not. Today she wore a dress and her mother's bonnet with her short hair tucked neatly inside. He would never guess. Would he?

Scarcely able to breathe, her heart fluttering like the wings of a small bird, she determined to behave like a proper young lady. Nothing at all like Albert. *Act like a lady!* Mother constantly reminded her. *Stand up straight! Don't walk with those great huge strides of yours! Don't interrupt! Don't argue about everything under the sun! Don't forget to smile!* And so Katherine squared her shoulders, lifted her chin, and started toward them taking small, elegant steps. She smiled graciously.

All went well until her boot sank into something quite ominously mushy. The warm, acrid smell that rose from it left no doubt. She glanced down. The bottom and sides of her leather boot were coated in a dark, sticky mixture from which little pieces of brown grass stuck out.

Aw. What was she supposed to do now? Certainly not laugh. Katherine pressed her lips together, raised her chin, and wondered how a lady was supposed to watch where her feet were stepping if she could not look down.

"Katrine!" Madame Landvoight said. "We have been looking for you. This is Monsieur Roebear, who has come to see your horse."

Oh. Madame Landvoight might pronounce his name quiet differently, but the man standing before her was still Mr. Charles Roberts, the storekeeper from Yale. If Katherine had known he was also the horse trader, she would not have come here today. She saw the surprise in his eyes and knew Mr. Roberts recognized her. He would be furious! This man had refused payment for Nugget because of Susan, and now here she was, trying to sell the very same horse back to him. He had every right to be angry.

Something else occurred to her then. Something that made her toes curl inside her boots. Mr. Roberts would tell Madame Landvoight about Katherine's visit to his store with William as her guide. Madame Landvoight would tell her husband and her husband would tell... well, it did not bear thinking about.

"I believe we have met before," Mr. Roberts said, extending his hand. "It's a great pleasure to see you again, Miss Harris. And your beautiful horse as well," he glanced down at Katherine's boot, "even if she is a trifle messy at times."

Katherine shook his hand and attempted a smile, not a gracious one perhaps, but any semblance of a smile would do. Mr. Roberts was being kind enough to keep her secret. She tried to come up with something lady-like to say in exchange but could only think, *Please don't mention William. My father never approved of our friendship.*

If Father finds out William was with me for part of my trip north, he'll be furious at me. Even worse, he will be angry at William, and for no good reason.

Mr. Roberts pulled at his thick brown mustache with a finger and thumb. "I assume you had a safe trip and were able to find your brother?"

"I, uh, yes, thank you." She felt the need to keep talking, anything to prevent him from mentioning her visit to his store last month. "George is safe at home and he's actually working hard for once in his life. He's digging the well now and will build a small barn for Duke and Genevieve – that's our horse and cow. It seems George works much better when Father doesn't hang over him and tell him what he's doing wrong every minute of the day."

Mr. Roberts threw back his head and laughed. He had a pleasant enough laugh, one that revealed a row of straight teeth below his mustache. Katherine was surprised to realize that this man was younger than she first thought. At a guess he was not more than three or four years older than her brother. "Ah, yes," he said, "that is a common behavior in young men. I remember my own father..." He paused and studied Katherine.

She shifted from one foot to the other, twisting Nugget's reins around her fingers.

"But that is not important now."

"I must go," Madame Landvoight told them. "I will leave you both to make the deal."

Katherine watched the storekeeper walk away. *Make the deal.* Her stomach collapsed. Nugget stepped closer and pressed her soft muzzle against Katherine's shoulder. The warmth and trust in that gentle touch made Katherine's eyes sting. She turned away from Mr. Roberts to run her fingers through the long black hair of Nugget's mane. She wanted to bury her face in it. She needed a means of escape. How could she possibly go through with this?

Time slowed down. Why was the man so quiet? Katherine was afraid to look. She never should have come here. She could never ask him to buy this horse, this gift. If only she had known.

"I understand you want to sell your horse."

"Oh." There. He said it for her. Katherine felt a sharp pain in her chest. She could not breathe. Could not answer. What to say? *Yes, thank you very much for giving me this beautiful horse but now I'd like to sell her, so how much will you pay me?*

Silence closed in around them. What now? Katherine wanted to speak, needed to look. What was he doing? She stole a sideways glance, hoping he would not notice. But he was watching her. She could scarcely believe it when he smiled.

"It's not that I want to sell her," she said, "because I really, really don't. Nugget is such a wonderful horse, but the problem is..." She hesitated.

"Your family needs the money?"

Katherine nodded.

"If you want to know what I think..."

Here it came. Now he would tell her what he really thought, that she had a lot of nerve coming here...

"I think you are a remarkably brave young woman."

Well, that was an unusual way of phrasing it, but still meant the same thing after all. She had a lot of nerve.

"I'm sorry, Mr. Roberts, but I didn't know you were the horse trader. Do you think I would have tried to sell Nugget back to you had I known?"

DAYLE CAMPBELL GAETZ

He looked confused. Cupped his hand under his chin. Rubbed his mustache. "Nugget is your horse, Miss Harris, to do with as you please."

"But..."

"Have you forgotten the reason I gave her to you? It was my way of thanking your sister, who, according to my older brother, saved the life of his baby when his little family was so ill aboard ship. Yes. Nugget is your horse and a fine horse too. I expect to make a good profit on her when I get to Victoria, so you mustn't worry that I'm doing you a favour. This is not charity, Miss Harris. We will both gain from the sale."

Katherine began to feel better. "I hadn't thought of that."

"As a matter of fact, I already have a buyer in mind. Only two days ago I was in Victoria speaking with the man who just last month got himself elected as the city's first mayor. He asked what I might have in stock to help him win the autumn horse races."

Katherine tried to picture William Cubitt, Lord Mayor of London, an old man with a white powdered wig on his head, racing around the track astride a horse. "Surely you don't mean he'll ride the horse *himself*?"

Mr. Roberts laughed at her surprise. "He will indeed. The mayor hates to lose any sort of competition and loves to race horses. That's why he's looking for a fast horse before the races begin."

"Then he's in luck. I know Nugget is fast. She had no trouble beating Duke in a horse race when George needed convincing to return home. Please never tell my brother, but Nugget wasn't even trying very hard."

"Yes, your Nugget is a fast horse, and strong too.

Being an unusually large man, the mayor needs a powerful horse to carry him and so will be willing to pay good
money. Shall we talk terms?"

Katherine nodded. She had a good idea of what Nugget was worth, her mother saw to that. *Now mind you don't
sell the horse unless you get your price for it,* she said before
Katherine left this morning.

So when Mr. Roberts made his offer, Katherine knew
it was more than fair. The two shook hands, sealing the
deal.

"Katrine! Monsieur Roebear!"

They turned to see Madame Landvoight at the edge
of the grassy field. Katherine waved and the storekeeper
started toward them.

"Please," Katherine ventured, "please don't mention
William."

Mr. Roberts studied her curiously. "William?"

"Yes, that young man who acted as my guide. My father, um, my father..." She fumbled for the right words.

"Doesn't approve of your associating with an Indian
boy?"

Now, how did he know that? She considered Mr. Roberts more closely. The man had an intriguing sort of face,
not handsome, but kind and humorous at the same time,
as if he would far sooner laugh than be angry.

"I only wanted a friend," she confided, "but William's
father didn't like me either, even though he never spoke
one word to me. When we arrived at William's village his
father watched us, all grumpy and disapproving, exactly
the way my own father would be. After that William told
me a man can't be friends with a girl. He sent me away."

"Sometimes the world can seem unfair," Mr. Roberts

agreed. "But I expect, with a pretty daughter such as yourself, your father won't relax until he has you safely married."

Katherine stared up at him, speechless. She was thankful Madame Landvoight arrived at that moment.

"Eh bien, you have concluded your business?"

When they assured her they had, Madame Landvoight said, "Please then, come to our store. I have made such a marvelous apple pie. But I must hurry now to take it from the oven." She scurried off without waiting for an answer.

The pie was hot and bubbling over with sweet, syrupy juices. When everyone was served, Katherine picked up her fork and sliced into the triangle of pie on her plate. A curl of vapour rose from it. She closed her eyes, breathing in the rich aroma. She tasted it and flavour burst into her mouth with such warm sweetness she closed her eyes again. "This is delicious!" she murmured, taking another bite.

Katherine could have eaten the entire pie but forced herself to eat like a lady, which meant taking dainty bites and saying, "No thank you," to a second slice when she really meant, "Yes, please."

Madame Landvoight winked at her and placed another slice on her plate anyway. Katherine nodded her thanks.

While they ate, seated around a plank table in the small kitchen behind the Landvoights' store, Mr. Roberts questioned Katherine about her family. She found herself telling him about their comfortable life in England, her family's successful shop, how lucky she had been to have a tutor and then attend a girls' school even if for only a year. "And then my father decided to sell the shop and move us to British Columbia."

"Why would your papa do such a thing?" Madame

Landvoight wanted to know. "Did your mama agree?"

Katherine took a small bite of pie and held it in her mouth while she considered what to say. She must not reveal too much about her family's personal affairs; that would be disloyal. How could she explain that Father was never content with what he had? Father had been convinced that the only way to better himself was to become a landowner. Of course he could never afford to buy a farm in England, where the landed gentry owned huge tracts of land passed down from one generation to another, so he dragged his entire family to this colony. If he pictured himself as a gentleman farmer collecting money from tenants who paid to work his land, imagine his shock when faced with acres of wilderness and no one but themselves to tame it.

"My mother was happy enough in England," she said at last. "And my brother too. They both longed to stay. But Susan and I were excited about moving here. We thought of it as a big adventure." She put down her fork. "We even discussed plans to open a little country school one day, just the two of us. Susan thought she already had enough education to do so."

Katherine pushed away her half-finished slice of pie. Its sweet aroma now made her feel sick. "Nothing turned out the way we had hoped. We were horribly seasick on the steamship across the Atlantic, all except Susan and George. By the time we crossed the isthmus by train and caught a ship to San Francisco, the entire family was so ill with Panama Fever we thought we would die. We had to stay in a hotel and pay a doctor for expensive medicines. Even so, my sister never recovered properly."

Katherine hesitated. The room fell silent around her.

She stared at her hands, folded in her lap. She took a quick breath. "Toward summer's end my brother decided he couldn't face a long winter on the farm. He thought if he went north to the Cariboo he could bring us back a fortune in gold. So Father gave him enough money for supplies and off he went."

She stumbled on for long enough to tell them about her father's injuries and the reason she needed to fetch her brother. "And now we don't have enough money to purchase supplies for winter," she finished.

No one spoke. Katherine could not look up, could not bear their sympathy. She could scarcely breathe around the painful lump in her throat.

"I must say," Mr. Roberts broke the silence at last, "my troubles seem minor compared to yours."

When no one responded, he continued on, making Katherine wonder if his words were meant to fill the void, giving her time to compose herself.

"For some time now I have longed to escape this wild colony and travel to my brother's plantation in Jamaica for a long visit. However, aside from the Landvoights here, who have a store of their own to run, there is no one in British Columbia I would trust to run my store and oversee my properties. It seems I'll be stuck here forever."

"Ah, oui," Madame Landvoight said. "Thousands of the young men have flocked to this land wit' their big dreams to become rich. Sadly, most have not found the gold and have no money to return home. Such a rowdy group is not to be trusted."

"Too many men and too few women makes for trouble," Monsieur Landvoight agreed. "What we need are more families like Katherine's who will settle the land

and spend their money in our stores."

"That may be true," Mr. Roberts said, "but I'm afraid it doesn't help me."

Katherine glanced up at him, a hint of an idea forming in her mind.

A few minutes later, the men walked outside while Katherine stayed behind to thank Madame Landvoight. Her hand was on the door, her mind busy exploring this unexpected idea, when Madame Landvoight said, "Charles Roebear is a charming young man, yes?"

Surprised, Katherine took a moment to consider. Charming? Maybe. He certainly was kind enough. But young? The man was well into his twenties. "I suppose he is," she said.

"Such a fine man deserves a good wife, no?"

"Uh...I guess so." Katherine scurried outside, pushing Madame Landvoight's words from her mind. She had more important matters to consider.

Monsieur Landvoight was heading for the stack of goods that had been unloaded from the sternwheeler. Mr. Roberts walked in the opposite direction, toward Nugget.

Katherine trudged along behind him, fighting tears. This was no time for self-pity. There was little enough time to sort out her thoughts. So she swallowed, straightened her shoulders and walked a little faster.

Mr. Roberts stopped several yards from Nugget, and Katherine scooted past him. She rubbed her knuckles against Nugget's broad forehead and looked into those trusting brown eyes. "I'm so sorry, girl," she whispered. She hoped Mr. Roberts would stay back, allowing her a few private moments to say her goodbyes.

"Miss Harris, it's time I settled my debt."

Startled, Katherine realized he was standing directly behind her.

"Thank you," she said, accepting the money. She waited, looking up at him, willing him to leave and yet wanting him to stay. She had something to say, if only she could work up the nerve.

Katherine shifted her weight from one foot to the other. Twisted at the money in her hands. Glanced over her shoulder at Nugget. Turned back to Mr. Roberts. Would he be angry? Men did not take kindly to a young girl offering suggestions of her own, she knew that, but Mr. Roberts seemed different somehow. He seemed...*charming*.

He cupped his chin in his hand, rubbing his fingers over his mustache and looking down at Katherine as if wondering why she was still here.

All right then. What was the worst that could happen? The man could say no. He could laugh at her. In truth she had nothing to lose. Katherine pressed her shoulders back and cleared her throat. "Mr. Roberts," she said, "I believe I know exactly the right people to run your store in your absence."

Mr. Roberts listened carefully and even offered a few suggestions of his own. They discussed the plan at some length, standing next to Nugget under warm September sunshine, until at last they shook hands in agreement. Then Katherine returned to the store while Mr. Roberts walked over to help Monsieur Landvoight with the supplies.

After paying Madame Landvoight what she was owed, Katherine left the store and once more climbed onto Nugget to hurry home. She took no delight in this unexpected final ride. Nugget was no longer hers and Katherine would just as soon have said her goodbyes and gotten it over with. But Mr. Roberts had insisted she take the horse and ride ahead to tell her parents they should expect company for tea.

"And what could this Mr. Roberts possibly want with us?" her father asked when Katherine told him.

"He has something important to discuss, but I'm not sure of the details. Perhaps we should leave it to him to explain."

Father's eyes narrowed in suspicion. "Katherine, you do understand that one day, when the time is right, your mother and I will look into finding an appropriate husband for you?"

Her mouth fell open. "Oh!" she gasped. "Oh, you think...?" Her cheeks burned. "Father, really, it is nothing like that. I'm only fourteen!"

"Girls younger than you have been brought by brideships to Victoria to marry the ruffians hanging about there and begin a civilized colony." He shrugged. "A wasted effort if you ask me, since those orphan girls are of the lowest class imaginable."

"Father, I have no intention of marrying, I assure you. If I had any choice in the matter I would continue my schooling – but of course that's impossible with the nearest school being in Victoria." There, she had done it, put the idea into his head just as she told Mr. Roberts she would do. Her father knew how much she had enjoyed her school in England, and it was his fault she couldn't finish.

Father winced and turned away. He limped toward the open door, looking so broken Katherine felt sorry for her words. "Father," she called after him, "Mr. Roberts has a business proposal he hopes to discuss with you. He believes you will like it."

Father continued out to the porch.

Mother was busy measuring flour, sugar, and salt. "This is such a surprise," she said. "No one ever visits us out here. Katherine dear, would you run out and gather some eggs for scones?"

As the sun sank lower in the sky, Katherine began to worry Mr. Roberts might not show up after all. Maybe he needed to catch a sternwheeler back to Yale. Maybe he had a change of heart. She filled a basket with potatoes and carted it to the root cellar beneath the lean-to kitchen at the back of their cabin. While there, she checked over the few buckets of apples she had picked earlier in the week from the young trees planted by the previous owners of this farm. There were also carrots, beets, onions, and turnips stored for winter. Not much was left in the garden now, but perhaps there would be enough food for one person to manage until spring.

When she emerged from the cellar, Katherine heard voices. She followed the sound to the front porch and found Mr. Roberts perched awkwardly on the thick chunk of log George had cut and placed there as a seat for himself. Her father was settled in their one outside chair, carved out of wood, where he spent so much of his time these days.

"Well, hello again, Miss Harris." Mr. Roberts rose politely when she stepped onto the porch.

She nodded at him and glanced at her father before settling on the top step, hoping to listen in, if not to offer any comments of her own. Her father would not be pleased if he learned she and Mr. Roberts had hatched this plan together.

"Perhaps you will help your mother in the kitchen?" Father suggested in that tone he used when he really meant, *Do as I say or else.*

Katherine hesitated. She glanced from Father to Mr. Roberts, who gave a slight nod of his head. Reassured, she stood up and slipped inside. Her mother was bustling about, her face flushed pink, making tea.

"Katherine dear, everything is almost ready. Could you finish for me while I go outside and talk with Mr. Roberts? He has something important to discuss with us."

While she set the table, Katherine strained to hear, but their voices were too low. When they came inside, none of their expressions gave anything away. George arrived, shaking his hands, wet from washing at the bucket outside. He sat with the men while Mother fetched the tea pot.

Katherine carried a jar of blackberry jam and a plate piled high with freshly baked scones. As she leaned over to place the plate on the table, she took the opportunity to glance sideways at her father. He turned to her, smiling as though all his cares had been lifted from his shoulders. "Mr. Roberts here has made us a proposal," he said. "It involves you."

Katherine glanced at Mr. Roberts, then quickly back to Father as if she couldn't wait to hear their news. She completely forgot the large plate in her hand until it began tipping in Mr. Roberts' direction. Before she could right it, a scone flew off and landed on his lap.

"Why, thank you Miss Harris." He placed the fat scone on his plate. "I believe I will have one. They smell delicious."

Her father looked puzzled. "Are you quite all right,

Katherine?"

"I'm fine." She sat down heavily. She must not laugh.

"Oh Katherine," Mother said, "just wait until we tell you. This is such an excellent opportunity for all of us."

"All of us?"

"Yes." Father pointed a jam-covered knife in her direction. "Katherine, how would you like to go to school in Victoria for the winter?"

"School?" She avoided looking at Mr. Roberts for fear she would give away too much of their plans. They had agreed to lead Father to believe school was his idea alone. She did not need to feign surprise though, because she was genuinely amazed that everything fell together so smoothly. "But doesn't school cost money?"

"We won't have enough money for an expensive private school. However, after the sale of Nugget and with... but we'll let Mr. Roberts explain," Mother said.

Mr. Roberts sipped his tea, rubbed his hands together, and began. "For some time now I have been wanting to visit my brother and his wife on their plantation in Jamaica and meet my little niece, Rose. I shall have more than enough money for my passage after I sell my horses in Victoria. However, I need someone competent to run my store while I'm gone. Until you told me of your family's background at the Landvoights' earlier today, I could think of no one to handle the job reliably and not drive my store into bankruptcy in my absence.

"As you explained, Miss Harris, your parents have vast experience of running a shop in England and your mother is rather adept at managing accounts. They assure me they would enjoy the company of being in a town this winter. At the same time they will make a profit from running the store, enough to pay for their keep and more besides."

He paused and looked directly at Katherine. "It was your father who suggested you might go to school."

"Really?" She turned to her father. He looked so pleased with himself, so happy to offer her this gift, that seeing him brought sudden tears to her eyes. "Oh Father, I don't know what to say."

"Katherine," he smiled at her, "this is a wonderful opportunity to improve your education and make new friends at the same time."

"Yes," she nodded. "Thank you so much!" She couldn't hold back then; she laughed out loud. She would escape the drudgery of life on this lonely farm. She would make new friends. She would learn new things.

She turned to George. His shoulders were hunched over. His scone, buttered and slathered with blackberry jam, lay forgotten on his plate. He stared at a bright shaft of sunlight slanting through the open door.

"George will need to remain on the farm, of course," Father said. "There is work to finish and Duke and Genevieve to care for. But there should be enough food for one person, even your brother. And he has friends he can visit in Hope."

"Poor George," Katherine said. "He's the one who longed to get away on a great adventure, and now he's the only one to be stuck on the farm."

"Yes," Father agreed, "but come spring when Mr. Roberts returns, perhaps George can still travel up to the Cariboo if he chooses."

"I suppose I can hang on until spring," George said, and bit into his scone.

"Then it's all settled." Mother looked happier than she

DAYLE CAMPBELL GAETZ

had since they left England. "I shall need to alter some frocks of..." She hesitated. She glanced at Katherine, her eyes filled with pain.

Katherine nodded. Her throat tightened and she stared down at her hands. She knew exactly what her mother could not say. Mother would shorten some of Susan's old frocks to fit Katherine.

Mother cleared her throat. "Do you remember that nice widow, Mrs. Morris, whom we met in Victoria? She was considering taking in a boarder to help pay expenses now that she is on her own."

Katherine remembered her all right, but she wouldn't call the woman nice. When Katherine had tried to ask her a question about Victoria, that woman had stuck her nose in the air and pretended not to hear. Then she had leaned toward Mother. "I have always believed children should be seen and not heard," she said in a loud whisper. "Don't you agree?"

"I'll write to her now," Mother said, "so Mr. Roberts can carry the letter back with him. And naturally I shall accompany you to Victoria when the time comes."

"Of course," Katherine agreed without enthusiasm. This was something she had not foreseen. Something bad to dampen the good. If attending school meant living with Mrs. Morris, could she manage? Could she keep her mouth shut and behave like a proper lady? Susan would have done so easily, Katherine knew that, but she wasn't at all sure about herself. She slid her hand into her pocket, found the cloth bag, and clutched the gold nugget between her thumb and forefinger.

She would learn to deal with Mrs. Morris, anything to get away from this farm and attend school.

Emma

Arrival of the Tynemouth – ... As a matter of course, we went aboard the steamer yesterday and had a good look at the lady passengers. They are mostly cleanly, pretty young women... Taken altogether, we are highly pleased with the appearance of the "invoice," and believe they will give a good account of themselves in whatever station of life they may be called on to fill – even if they marry lucky bachelor miners from Cariboo.

– The British Colonist, September 19, 1862

4

Even after all these months, Emma still hesitated every single morning, afraid to open her eyes for fear this new life of hers would turn out to be a dream. Snatched away like it never was real at all. For certain-sure she would wake up on the gritty floor of that squalid little room, curled up tight on a thin straw mattress, shivering with an awful cold that seeped into her very bones. Close beside Emma, her poor mam would be wasting away with disease while both of them longed for a crust of bread to ease their aching hunger.

This morning, the memory of that closet-sized room was so strong Emma tasted the bitter grit of coal dust on her tongue and smelled the stink of open sewers in the streets of Manchester. She shivered in the chill of early morning. Was it true then? Was it out there, waiting for her the very second she opened her eyes? Was her beautiful dream over and the nightmare of real life returned?

Emma half opened one eye, no more than a crack, but the room was solid black around her. She opened both eyes wide and listened in the darkness for the terrifying wheeze of her mother's breathing. Nothing. Not a sound but the distant rumble of a steam engine.

She allowed herself to hope now, allowed her body to

curl into the big, soft mattress. The fear in her belly eased, the quick pounding of her heart slowed to normal. But a stink of coal still hung in the air, and an icy draft from the window made her shiver. She felt around in the dark, found the heavy Hudson's Bay blanket crumpled beside her on the bed, pulled it over her head and snuggled deep beneath it.

Emma smiled in her dark cocoon because her dream was still alive. She was still here, in this brand new little city, safe in the Douglas family home, where there was always food enough for everyone, even a servant-girl such as herself. Wouldn't she just love to lie here all morning, so deliciously warm now under her blanket? So content.

So lazy! That annoying little voice piped up inside her head. *Lie here all day and see if you don't lose your job. Mrs. Douglas, kind as she is, would tell you to pack your things and be off. Could be she'd make you leave behind those dresses she altered to fit your tall, scrawny frame. Those few dresses Alice Douglas never did manage to smuggle out before she ran off and got herself married at seventeen.*

Lose this job and where will you go then?

Emma stuck her head out from beneath the warm blanket. She would have no choice but to move in with Joe Bentley. Maybe Tall Joe really was her father, like he said, but that didn't mean she had to move into his house. Emma knew all about fathers. Fathers made you follow a whole string of rules made only to suit their own selves. One mistake and they kicked you out the door and pretended they never did have a daughter at all.

That's what happened to her mam and would happen to her too if she didn't watch out. Come spring, and all goes well, she still planned on going off with Tall Joe and his cousin to start that farm in British Columbia he was forever going on about. She told him she would, and that's a fact. But she never did promise. If that Tall Joe started telling her what to do, she still might change her mind, and that's for certain-sure. Beneath the blanket she touched her fingertips to her ring, felt the smooth roundness of it. Usually the ring brought comfort. Today it only made her angry.

Emma tossed off the blanket and slid out of bed. The cold floor was a shock to her bare feet. A gust of icy wind blew through the wide open window and she hurried over to close it. She paused there, hands on the sash. High above the bare and twisted twigs of Garry oaks a million stars glittered in an ink-black sky. A fresh blast of frigid air chilled her face and arms.

It was the stink that woke her up, the same thick, choking coal smell that filled every drop of air in Manchester. Not near so bad here, Emma thought. Here it was no more than a hint of coal dust on a clean, crisp breeze. The smell would be blowing this way from the harbour, with all the steamers anchored there. She slammed the window down and locked it tight.

She felt around the dressing table, found her candle and lit it. Its pale glow chased all the shadows into dark corners of her attic bedroom. Emma dressed quickly by its light. So long as she kept her job with Governor and Mrs. Douglas, she would have a room of her own and never go hungry again.

Emma wound her long, dark braids around the top of her head and pinned them in place. She paused to study her pale, narrow face in the tiny hand mirror. She would be fourteen years old next spring and didn't need some father looking after her, as Tall Joe seemed to think. After Mam died, didn't Emma stay clear of the workhouse, like she promised? Didn't she spend three long months cooped up with all those other poor girls in the hold of a steamship with rats and cockroaches for company? If she survived all that, she positively could take care of her own-self in this wild little colony of Vancouver's Island.

Her candle cast an eerie light on the narrow stairway as Emma made her way down. With every step, her right hip ached and her knee felt as if a nail was being driven into it. Emma almost cried, the pain was that sharp. But worse, she was angry to feel it come back on her after all this time. It was the cold, she knew. Cold always made the pain worse.

Emma limped into the huge kitchen, where she lit a lantern and stoked up the fire in the woodstove. Then she set about making breakfast. By the time Mrs. Douglas appeared, the kitchen was warm, hot porridge bubbled on the woodstove, and the pain had eased up. Emma's limp was barely noticeable.

By mid-afternoon, with the lunch dishes done and the house cleaned until it sparkled, Emma fetched a broom and hurried outside. She started sweeping the long, narrow verandah, where thousands of crisp brown oak leaves collected in great drifts. That cold dry wind still blew, rushing in from the northeast instead of Victoria's more usual damp but mild southwest wind. Emma smiled as she tackled the leaves. Even if the cold bit at her nose and ears, it didn't seep through to her bones. It didn't make her shiver from the inside out, not like back in England, where she lived most days with her stomach so empty it ached and she hadn't so much as a pair of shoes to warm her feet.

She might still be thin, but not so half-starved as the day she stepped off that horrible ship. And now she had this lovely warm cloak Mrs. Douglas had given her to replace her thin shawl that never did keep out the wind or rain.

Emma made a neat pile of leaves on the verandah, then swept them down, one step at a time, to the sidewalk. She had no sooner finished than an extra strong gust whipped into the pile and sent a cloud of leaves twisting and swirling back up to the verandah.

"Well an' wouldn't you just know it." Emma stopped working and leaned on the broom. "All that work an' what's the use?"

"If you ask me, you're fighting a losing battle here, my girl," a voice said from close behind.

Emma froze. She knew that voice. And just like him to come sneaking up, chuckling in his beard, and her talking to herself like she was daft. Emma whirled around. "Well, Tall Joe, an' just wot're you doin' here, then? I gots work to do, don't you know."

Tall Joe winced. Emma knew he hated her talking that way, using the language she picked up on the streets of Manchester, reminding him how much she and her mother had suffered while he was off having his great adventure in the new world. She watched his eyes cloud over with hurt, and her anger grew. There was something inside her, something uncontrollable that built up so strong and fast it had to be set loose or she would burst in two. She leaned on the broom and glared up at the man.

Joseph Bentley might want her to call him Father, but the word would never pass her lips, not after more than thirteen years of believing he was dead. Still and all, "Mr. Bentley" sounded much too formal. So she had settled on "Tall Joe" whether he liked it or not. That was the name they called him up in the Cariboo where he found himself a fortune in gold. And that's the name she would call him.

"You shouldn't ever come by when I'm workin', Tall Joe," she reminded him. "You'll have me losin' my job and be stuck with me day and night, like it or not."

"I wouldn't mind that, Emma," he said softly.

"You can say that well enough, but we'd be sick of each other inside of a week."

"Not if you go to school."

Emma dropped the broom over a pitifully small pile of leaves and started up the steps, fists clenched tight at her sides. Anger pressed hard against her ribs, bursting to get out. Didn't they have this argument two times before? The man had a problem with his head, and that's for certain-sure. Couldn't remember what a person told him or couldn't understand it, one of the two. She would never go to school. Not now, not at her great age, and she'd never been to a real school in her whole entire life. Even little Martha Douglas, who attended school every day, could read better than her, and she only a child of eight.

No, Emma did not need any of that. Them sitting at their little desks, laughing at her for being such a great, huge fool. She grabbed the front door handle.

"Emma, please, I'm sorry. I know I promised not to bring it up again, but I still think you'd like to be able to read and write." He paused, and when she didn't answer but stood facing the door with her back straight and shoulders tense, he added more gently, "I'm simply trying to be a father to you."

She turned and glared down at him, eyes blazing.

"An' didn't I tell you I don't need takin' care of?"

"Yes, you did."

"I can take care of me own-self."

"Yes, you can."

"Then why do you keep after me about goin' to school, I'd like to know?"

Tall Joe studied her face, he rubbed a hand over his thick brown beard and his dark eyes looked up at Emma with a hint of pain in them. "It won't happen again, I promise. Just let me know if you change your mind, will you?"

Emma shrugged.

"Meanwhile, I have something to show you. Something I know you'll like."

She waited, but he said nothing more. "What is it then?"

"Tomorrow is Wednesday, your half day off, correct?" She nodded.

"I'll come by for you at one o'clock."

With that he swung around and strode down the straight sidewalk as fast as he could go without running.

"An' I never said I'd go with yer!" she called after him.

He laughed, turned his head, and called over his shoulder, "You're going to love it!"

"Not if I can help it!"

He laughed again.

Emma limped back down the stairs to fetch the broom. And what was so funny, she'd like to know.

At noon the following day, Emma picked up the large, steaming kettle that always sat on the woodstove. As she

DAYLE CAMPBELL GAETZ

made tea she thought about Tall Joe. He said he'd fetch her at one o'clock but never bothered to ask if she had plans of her own. If she drank her tea and gobbled her food fast enough, she could be gone before he showed his face. Could be she'd take a stroll up to Beacon Hill or walk through town an' gape in shop windows at all the expensive goods she never could afford in a lifetime of work.

Mrs. Douglas walked into the kitchen with a wide smile on her broad and friendly face. Eight-year-old Martha and eleven-year-old James, the only two Douglas children at home since Alice eloped last year, spent their days at school, and Governor Douglas was always off doing whatever he did every day over at those Birdcages of his. So there were only the two of them at home come noon.

Emma always felt comfortable with Mrs. Douglas. Her employer was not like those other ladies who flitted about town in their foolish hoop skirts and thought they were better than anyone else, just because they were British and not from the working class. Those ladies in their fancy dresses turned up their noses when Emma walked by, and they didn't much like Amelia Douglas either, even if she was the governor's wife. They didn't care how nice she was; they looked down on her because her mother was Cree and not from good British stock.

There was a quiet sadness about Mrs. Douglas. Most people thought she felt out of place in a British society such as Victoria, but Emma wasn't so sure. She thought her employer still missed all those babies of hers who died. Mrs. Douglas sometimes talked of them to Emma. Of thirteen babies, only six were still alive and the four older girls had married and left home. Mrs. Douglas loved being a mother and treated Emma almost as another daughter.

"Ah, Emma, I'm glad you've made tea. Now if you slice some of that bread we made this morning, I'll get cheese and cold chicken to eat with it."

A few minutes later, when they were seated at the kitchen table, Mrs. Douglas said, "You seem in a big hurry today, Emma. Did you make plans for your afternoon off?"

Emma chewed on a mouthful of bread and cheese. She swallowed and took a great gulp of tea. "Nothing special," she said.

"Emma, a girl your age needs friends. Why not pay a visit to that girl you knew on the *Tynemouth?* Mary works for Mrs. Steeves now, which isn't far to walk."

Well, she never would go near Mrs. Steeves' house, and that's for certain-sure. Last time she saw Mrs. Steeves, that woman called her a poor wretch from the brideship, *Tynemouth,* who was too much of a troublemaker to catch herself a husband. Then she had carried on insulting Mrs. Douglas until Emma couldn't help but toss back a few words of her own.

"Mary isn't my friend." Emma sipped her tea and avoided looking at Mrs. Douglas. "She's only someone I knew aboard ship."

And Emma never did need a friend. Start caring about someone and they up and died on you like Elizabeth Buchanan. She shuddered, remembering how all the brideship girls had been locked in the hold of the *Tynemouth* when it stopped at the Falkland Islands. Emma had watched through the port hole as her only friend's coffin, small and cheaply made, was carried to shore and disappeared from view.

DAYLE CAMPBELL GAETZ

Mrs. Douglas gazed steadily at Emma for what seemed a very long time but didn't ask any more questions. That was the best thing about Mrs. Douglas – she never pried. And if Tall Joe showed up later and Emma wasn't here, she'd never tell Emma it was rude to run off like that.

Even if it was.

And if I run off, I might never know what surprise Tall Joe has for me.

"Or could be I'll just wait and see if Tall Joe shows up. He said he might come by at one. 'Course, he might not. He might find something better to do."

"If he told you he would be here, then he will," Mrs. Douglas said confidently. "You must not worry so much, Emma. Tall Joe is not going to run off and desert you just because you start to like him."

Emma shifted uneasily on her chair. She looked past Mrs. Douglas and out the little square of a back window. The sun was shining, but the temperature hung around freezing.

They had not yet finished their meal when someone knocked on the front door.

"That must be Mr. Bentley," Mrs. Douglas said. "Ask him if he'd like to have a cup of tea with us."

"No, must be someone else." Emma got up from the table. "It's too soon for Tall Joe."

"He is wise to come early." Mrs. Douglas, being a woman who never wasted words, said nothing more.

She didn't need to. Emma understood exactly what the older woman meant. Emma left the warm kitchen and walked down a drafty hall to the front door. She told herself that whoever stood on the other side of that door, would for certain-sure, not be Tall Joe. As for this surprise he went on about, she didn't trust it. Not at all. Who had ever, in her whole entire life, surprised her with something good?

The textile mill in Manchester surprised her by shutting down just when she needed money most; her mother surprised her by taking sick and dying; Mrs. Barnes surprised her by sending her off to this wild colony, and Elizabeth surprised her by dying before the ship got halfway here. Now Tall Joe had a surprise of his own. She tried to imagine what it could be and decided he must have enrolled her in school in spite of what he had said.

Emma trembled a little as she pulled open the door. Like as not she'd see some messenger come to say Mr. Bentley could not make it today. *Something came up. So terribly sorry, but maybe next week if nothing better happens along.*

But there he stood, his dark brown hair, the very same shade as her own, neatly combed and a big grin stuck in the middle of his full brown beard. Emma was a tall girl, but she had to put her head back to look up at his face in spite of his standing one whole step down from floor level.

"You're early!" she accused.

"I didn't want to miss you," he said. "I was afraid you might forget and go off to do something else."

"Don't think I didn't consider it."

"Emma," Mrs. Douglas came up behind her, "don't leave poor Mr. Bentley standing on the porch and all the warm air whooshing out the door. Invite him in for tea."

"That is very kind of you, Mrs. Douglas," he said, stepping inside. "But I mustn't stay long, I'm taking Emma

DAYLE CAMPBELL GAETZ

out to show her something and we'll need plenty of time before dark."

Emma shut the door and followed them to the kitchen. Was the man daft? There was a good long time until dark, and Victoria wasn't so big you couldn't walk the length of it and back again in under an hour.

5

"What's this then?" Emma stopped at the sidewalk's end, where a horse and cart stood waiting. She eyed the horse warily, careful to stand well back. Horses were not to be trusted.

"Your carriage, Madam," Tall Joe replied with a courteous bow and a mischievous wink.

"An' why should I need a carriage when I've got two good feet to take me where I want to go?"

"Because, Emma, we have a distance to cover and I want to get there as fast as possible."

"An' where can we go that the wheels won't sink in mud to their axles, I'd like to know?"

Tall Joe sighed and pressed his hand against his forehead. "Did no one ever say that you ask too many questions, my girl? If you must know, I am betting that with the clear skies and cold temperatures of the past few days, mud will no longer be a problem. If the ground isn't frozen at least it won't be filled with huge puddles."

Emma was about to tell him he was wrong when the horse, an ugly beast with a short black mane that stood up on end like a scrub brush, turned its head and studied her through two slits of evil brown eyes. Emma stopped breathing and glared into those eyes, determined not to show her fear.

The horse stretched its neck toward her and curled its upper lip, baring a row of square, yellow teeth. Emma jumped back. Horses were nasty, stubborn, violent creatures. Everyone knew that. She once saw a street urchin run over by a horse and carriage in Manchester, and the driver never so much as slowed down to see if the child was alive or dead.

And you never could tell when a horse would take it into its fool head to go galloping like a wild beast through the streets, tossing passengers out on the cobblestones and knocking street folk onto their backsides. And if that wasn't enough, they were dirty, smelly beasts, dropping great stinking gobs of mess to wash into gutters with all the disgusting muck of the streets.

"Look, Emma, he likes you," Tall Joe said. "He's looking for an apple." He reached into the big pocket of his coat. "Here, give him this."

Emma watched the horse strain its neck toward her. Its great flat teeth gnashed together as if the beast wanted to chomp down a finger or two. She took another step back, and her eyes shifted to the perfect, round apple that rested on the palm of Tall Joe's outstretched hand.

Emma's mind whisked back to a busy street corner with her shivering in her thin shawl, her bare feet cold on the cobblestones. "Apple, Sir?" "Apple, Ma'am?" she asked. And all those rich folk looked the other way, scurrying past a thin, hungry girl trying to sell apples and earn enough money to keep her poor mother alive. No matter how hungry she got, Emma never once could afford the luxury of biting into an apple. Not until she arrived in Victoria two months ago.

"What? An' you'd waste good food on a beast like that?"

Tall Joe studied her for a moment and then pulled out a small knife. He sliced the apple into pieces and began feeding them to the horse. "You see? He's very gentle, Emma. There's no need to be afraid of him."

"I'm not afraid of anything," Emma informed him, but quietly, so as not to attract attention from the animal.

"Glad to hear it." Tall Joe put the knife away. "Now, we'd better be going. Let me help you up."

Emma eyed the narrow seat looming above her. She felt herself tumbling from it. She would hit the hard earth with a great thud, land on her weak, twisted leg, and lie there helpless to get up.

Tall Joe saw the look on her face. "Have you never ridden on a cart before, Emma?"

"'Course I have." But she couldn't imagine how she was expected to climb to that narrow seat and, once there, keep herself from falling off.

"All right then, simply put your foot right here and up you go."

Emma allowed him to take her arm and help her, but only because she had no idea how she was expected to do such a thing and did not fancy looking like a fool. While Tall Joe supported her right elbow, Emma stepped up with her left leg, pulled with her left arm, and somehow managed to land in the seat without tripping over her long skirt. Tall Joe climbed beside her. He picked up the reins and flicked them lightly over the horse's back. "Giddyup, Jack!"

"Jack? You call the horse Jack?"

"Why not? Jack is a perfectly good name."

"For a man, maybe. Not for a horse."

The horse began to walk and the cart rattled forward on the uneven dirt road. The seat bounced and swayed to one side. "Oh!" Emma cried and clutched the edge of it. Something must be wrong. And the cart must be broken. It couldn't be meant to joggle a person about like a ship in a storm-tossed sea.

"I'm glad this isn't new to you," Tall Joe commented.

"Yes," she breathed. She looked down at her fingers, curled around the wooden seat until every knuckle showed as white as her opal ring. Her teeth were clenched so tight she felt a muscle twitch in her jaw and knew Tall Joe could see it.

"Some people are nervous on their first ride," he added.

"I expect they are."

The narrow wheels creaked onto James Bay Bridge and the cart swayed side to side. Emma gawked over the railing, down at dark, smelly mud left behind by the tide. She knew what would happen if this fool of a horse took it into its head to bolt. The cart would tip for certain-sure. It would hit the railing and out she would fly, flapping her arms and legs like a great, fat bird. She would land with a splat in that thick, slimy mud below.

Emma sat rigid with fear. She held her breath and clutched the seat while Jack plodded along until at last the wheels of the cart rolled off the bridge. The cart continued down a busy Victoria street, past brick buildings with tall, narrow archways above their windows and doors. Groups of men stood about on wooden sidewalks discussing worldly affairs, as men do.

Emma would bite her tongue clean off before saying so, but Tall Joe was right; the streets were not nearly so muddy as they had been last week, when the rains seemed never to stop. The cart passed through town and crossed over the bridge to Esquimalt Road. Emma began to feel more confident. She was getting used to the cart's sway and was not so afraid of tumbling off at any moment.

By now she had a different problem. The ground was hard and rocky. The cart wheels bounced over it and jolted Emma up and down until her backside ached. And it didn't help her sore hip either. Wouldn't she just love to get down and walk a ways, stretch her legs and warm up at the same time? She was that cold, sitting here like a great lump with nothing to do but watch the trees pass by.

The cart bounced down a slope to a low-lying area where the ground was wet and mucky. "The mud's bad here," she said.

Tall Joe didn't answer.

"It gets worse close to Esquimalt Harbour," she reminded him.

Still he didn't answer. He flicked the reins as the cart wheels sank deeper into the mud.

"Seems I could get down and walk faster'n this," she told him. "An' the poor horse strainin' to drag us along."

"Emma..." Whatever Tall Joe was about to say was interrupted when the cart settled quietly into a large mud puddle and came to a stop.

"Well then, here's your chance," he said.

She eyed him warily.

"So? Don't you want to get down and walk?"

A sea of brown water surrounded the cart. Little waves rippled across its surface after being disturbed by the wheels.

"Well, an' is this your surprise then?" she asked.

"Wadin' in a great mucky lake and ruinin' my boots?"

Tall Joe stared at her. His eyes narrowed, his mouth twitched. Emma waited for him to say something cross, tell her to climb down and walk home if that was the way she felt. So she was shocked when he threw back his head and laughed. "Yes," he said, "and how do you like it for a surprise?"

"Not so much, Tall Joe." The man must be daft, laughing when nothing was funny.

They both climbed out to lighten the load. Tall Joe guided the horse's head, and they were soon out of the puddle and moving again.

The second time they had to climb down, Emma looked sadly at her wet, muddy boots and the soggy, brown hem of her mud-spattered skirt. She stood aside and watched Tall Joe strain to help Jack pull out the wagon, sunk almost to its axles in soft mud.

"Seems like it would be faster to walk than dig ourselves out every two minutes," Emma observed.

Tall Joe didn't reply.

By the time they arrived at Craigflower, both were cold, wet, and muddy. They were also tired and not in the best of moods. Emma wondered why Tall Joe brought her here. She looked up at the big, square building with its two rows of windows. Could be it was a school. She turned to confront Tall Joe.

"It was worth all the trouble to get here," he said, climbing down from the seat. "As you will soon see."

He helped her down, tied Jack's reins to a hitching post, then guided Emma toward a wide, fenced-in field. Several horses grazed on a grassy slope beneath two wide-spreading Garry oaks.

"Do you see that beautiful bay mare with a long black mane and tail?" Tall Joe asked.

Emma nodded, even though she wasn't sure which one he meant. What did she know one horse from the other or care either?

A wide smile spread over Tall Joe's face. "She's yours!"

Emma frowned. "'Course she's not mine! Don't you think I would know it? An' why should I want a horse anyhow, great noisy, filthy beasts that they are? If ever I did own a horse I'd..." The look on Tall Joe's face made Emma cut the rest of her sentence off.

I'd sell it and keep the money. That's what she wanted to say, but Tall Joe looked so hurt Emma couldn't help but feel sorry for him. "Oh," she said with a quick intake of breath, "that's not your surprise?"

He nodded. "I thought you would like her, Emma. Most youngsters would love to have a horse of their own."

Emma didn't remind him she was most definitely not a youngster and would thank him not to call her one. She only shook her head and stared at the horses, wondering whatever possessed him to buy one for her.

She soon found out.

"You will need a good, strong horse when we travel up to the interior next spring. The trail is long and rugged, and we will be carrying all of our possessions. Between now and then, you and the horse will have time to get to know one another."

A horse. It never once occurred to Emma she might need a horse.

"And you'll want a horse to get around once we're living up there. We will likely be several miles from the nearest town."

DAYLE CAMPBELL GAETZ

Well, and if the need to ride a horse wasn't reason enough to change her mind about going, Emma didn't know what was. But she couldn't tell him now that she might not go. He looked too disappointed already.

She watched a hired hand set off toward the horses, carrying a circle of stout rope. He selected one of them, a shiny dark brown horse with a thick black mane and tail and long slender legs. He looped the rope over the horse's neck and patted it on the shoulder. The horse followed him. It looked almost like dancing, the way it lifted each hoof so high off the ground as it pranced toward the fence.

"This is her, then," the hired hand said. "Ain't she a beauty? An' she's fast too. She's the very same horse the mayor rode to win that race at Beacon Hill."

"I remember." Emma had watched the race with Edward, and the two of them had marveled that the poor horse could hold so much weight and still run so fast. "This horse must be very strong."

The man laughed. "She is that, but Mayor Harris sold her in spite of it. He says she's too good an animal to wear out with overburdening."

"He's right about that. The poor horse looked like a small pony under the weight of Tom Harris! I'd wager our mayor must weigh a good three hundred pounds." Tall Joe pulled another apple from his pocket and offered it to Emma.

She glanced from the apple to the horse. Standing so close made her tremble inside. "You give it to her," she said.

Tall Joe cut the apple in sections and offered them one by one to the horse. It took each one gently from his hand, chewed noisily, and reached for another. When there was only one piece left, Tall Joe tried again to hand it to Emma. "There's no need to be afraid, Emma. She's a very gentle horse."

"I'm not afraid," Emma insisted, and immediately wished she hadn't. The two men watched her, Tall Joe with his hand stretched toward her, a section of apple held between his fingers. Emma took it from him.

"All right then, Emma, simply step up to the fence and offer it to her. She won't hurt you, I promise."

With them watching she couldn't go running off, much as she'd like to. She took a half step closer and stretched out her arm, holding the slice of apple by its very tip. On the far side of the fence the horse stretched out its neck toward the apple. Just inches away now, Emma felt the warm, moist breath of the horse on her hand.

"Oh!" The apple slice dropped, and Emma bent to pick it up. When she looked again at the horse, two huge brown eyes stared back at her. There was a sparkle in them that made Emma feel certain the horse was laughing at her. "Think I'm scared, do you?" she asked. She tried again. Stretching her arm, she held only the smallest tip of the apple slice and leaned forward as far as she could.

The horse stretched out its neck, bared its teeth. The apple fell into the dirt, and this time Emma left it there.

"She likes you, Emma," Tall Joe said.

Emma thought that was the stupidest thing she'd heard all day and opened her mouth to tell him so.

"Will you want her saddled?" the hired hand asked.

Emma's mouth snapped shut. She felt suddenly ill.

"We won't worry about riding the horse today, thank you," Tall Joe told him. "If you could simply slip a bridle on her and put the sidesaddle in the cart, we'll lead the horse back to town."

"I thought you'd be pleased," Tall Joe grumbled on the way home. "Most girls would be grateful for a horse of their own. Your mother rode from the time she was small."

Emma felt a quick burst of anger. "My mother grew up in the countryside," she reminded him, "where her father was a parson. All a pauper girl in Manchester knows of horses is that it's worth her life to keep out of their way."

Tall Joe fell silent. They had crossed the bridge from Esquimalt and were passing back through town before he spoke again. "I found a place near town to board her," he said. "With a few lessons you'll be an expert horsewoman in no time."

Emma didn't believe a word of it. She turned around on the seat to be sure the horse was still there, still following along. She almost hoped it would be gone, escaped and run off to the farm where it came from. But that wouldn't do much good. Tall Joe would only fetch it back again.

Her attention was caught by something beyond the horse. Standing perfectly still at the side of the road and watching them pass was a girl about her own age. Her light brown hair was mostly hidden by a large bonnet. She wore a warm but simple cloak and a skirt that did not stick out like a bell, as many of the ladies in Victoria wore, but fell in soft folds to the tops of her leather boots. Clutched under one arm was a small stack of books, but it was the expression on the girl's face that made Emma take notice.

She seemed completely unaware of Emma and Tall Joe but followed every movement of the horse tied behind their cart. And her eyes looked uncommonly bright. They shone as if they were filled with tears.

The girl didn't glance one way or the other but took several steps onto the road, her free arm stretched toward the horse. Half running, the girl followed behind the cart. She cried out, but her words were lost in the creaking of wheels and the clip-clop of hoofbeats. The horse heard, though, and its ears perked up. It tried to turn its head but the reins were too taut. It tried to stop and half-stumbled as the force of the moving cart pulled it along. Agitated, the horse raised its head and whinnied. At this the girl stopped following and covered her mouth with her hand. Her face crumpled.

Emma turned away, shaking her head. Nothing of what she had seen made one jot of sense. It seemed everyone in this entire colony, except herself and Mrs. Douglas, was completely daft.

6

Emma leaned her forearms on the fence top, her eyes fixed on the muddy ground below. She would not look up. Tall Joe might have forced her to come here, but she never would pretend to be happy about it. Her whole entire day was ruined because of him.

She had only one full day off a week, and half of that was taken up by going to church – Governor Douglas saw to that. Now, instead of a few hours to do as she pleased, she had to waste her Sunday afternoon in this dreary stable yard with rain about to teem down at any minute, by the look of those dark clouds hanging over the treetops.

A hint of movement, a heavy footstep, and her eyes flicked to the barn door. Edward stepped out, leading that dreadful horse into the yard. And he called himself her friend! From the corner of her eye she watched the tall, gangly young man but refused to look directly at him. She was that cross.

Edward wore his work clothes and no hat, leaving his thick, light brown hair free to curl down to his eyebrows and over his ears. As near as Emma could figure, Edward was close to sixteen. His arms dangled awkwardly at his sides when he walked, as if he couldn't think what to do with them. His legs looked so loose at the knees they might wobble off in the wrong direction if he didn't pay close attention.

As if he knew she was watching, Edward suddenly flashed one of his wide-toothed smiles in her direction. His round, blue eyes twinkled in that friendly way of his that always made it difficult to stay cross at him. Emma stared at the mucky ground and pretended not to see.

A great loud snort from the horse sent a chill through her bones. Her head jerked up, and her heart took a quick extra beat. No more than ten feet away the beast stretched its long neck, lifted its nose to snuffle the air, shook its head from side to side, and refused to budge. Edward pulled at the reins, but the horse dug its hind feet into the thick, wet earth. In a gentle tone, Edward tried to coax it forward. "Come," he said, "meet our Emma. I know you'll like her."

"Don't you dare come one step closer," Emma warned, even though it seemed the horse didn't want to meet her any more than she wanted to meet it. Emma backed away from the fence. And just in time too, because that huge beast snorted and reared up on its hind legs.

She expected Edward to drop the reins and run for the fence as fast as he could move. He would give a great leap over it and land in a heap of arms and legs at her feet. And it would serve him right for helping Tall Joe. Even better, if he got a good swift kick in his hindquarters to speed him on his way.

To her amazement, Edward did not run but only tightened the reins. He spoke softly to the horse. When the horse settled its front feet on the ground, Edward ran his fingers gently through its thick mane, still speaking quiet words. The horse turned its huge head toward

Edward, upper lip curled. Emma held her breath, waiting for him to get a good nip on the shoulder, and that would serve him right too. Her mouth fell open when the horse uttered a soft grunt that sent a puff of moisture floating into the cool, damp air. Edward kept up his gentle talk and rubbed the animal's neck. After another moment, that wild beast stood stone still.

A movement near the barn door caught Emma's attention and she turned to look. Tall Joe. He nodded in her direction, happy to see her. She looked away.

"She's a beauty all right." Edward spoke only loud enough that Tall Joe and Emma could hear, careful not to frighten the horse. "A little skittish at first, but she's calm enough now." He turned from Tall Joe to Emma and flashed that annoying smile of his. "Emma," he said, "climb on over here and come meet your horse. Your father's asked me to teach you how to ride."

"Oh, and s'pose someone asks me what I think?" Emma grumbled, but the horse gave a loud snort and no one heard her. She was angry enough to spit and even angrier because no one so much as took notice.

Tall Joe walked toward her with slow, deliberate steps so as not to startle the horse. "You'll be safe enough in the yard here," he said softly, just as Edward had spoken to the horse. He extended his hand. "Come on, Emma, climb over the fence and I'll help you up while Edward holds the reins."

Up? Up where? Not on top of that great snorting, stomping, stinking beast, and that's for certain-sure! *Just come on over to Beckley Farm and have a good look at the horse. Get to know her slowly. You'll grow to like her soon enough, I'm certain of it. She's a beautiful animal and as good-natured as they come.*

That's what Tall Joe had said yesterday. And now look at him standing there, grinning through his beard and flashing those great, glaring eyes of his – and him holding out his hand, thinking she'd go climbing up on that animal just 'cause he wanted her to. Well, he could think about it some more, and Edward could too.

And she didn't know which one made her more cross. Tall Joe for asking Edward to teach her how to ride or Edward for agreeing. Neither one bothered to ask if she wanted to learn. Well, turned out she didn't, and that's for certain-sure.

"Emma," Tall Joe said, "if it's your crippled leg you're worried about, you don't need to climb the fence. You can walk round through the barn."

Crippled. Emma curled her fingers around the top fence rail. She glared at Tall Joe, too angry to speak. She was not a cripple, not like all those pauper children crawling under great dusty machines from the time they were small and their bones so soft they never did grow right. All those children who couldn't so much as walk by the time they finished growing, and no one had any use for them after that. Leave them to starve on the streets, that's what happens to cripples. Step around them and pretend they aren't even there.

Well, and she wouldn't let that happen to her and didn't need anyone feeling sorry for her either. Them thinking she was worthless and couldn't take care of her own-self.

Oh, but that saddle! It had only one stirrup, dangling down the horse's left side below a brace meant to hold the rider's upper leg. Above that, close to where a saddle horn

DAYLE CAMPBELL GAETZ

should be, were two short handles, curved like a cow's horns. Emma cringed, staring up at them. She imagined sitting up there, her right leg bent and cramped near the horse's neck. Her leg ached just thinking about it.

"Emma?"

Her eyes rolled to Tall Joe. His hand still out, he waited to help her over the fence. She focused on that hand, the long thin fingers stretched toward her, curved slightly upward, the creases on his palm like lines on an oak leaf. "Don't you go callin' me a cripple, Tall Joe," she said, her voice cold. "Just 'cause my leg might ache with the cold and damp."

"Look, Emma, I didn't mean..."

"An' you said to come and look at the horse. Get to know her slowly, is what you said."

"I did," he agreed. "Yes. But I thought..."

"I can see well enough from here," Emma told him. "An' if that's as good natured as they come, then I hope never to meet up with a bad-natured one."

Tall Joe dropped his hand. "All right then." His voice was tight with anger. "I'll have Edward lead the horse over to you."

Before she could object, Edward covered the short distance, bringing that great huge beast up against the fence. "She's beautiful, Emma. And she rides so smooth you'll think you're in a rocking chair. No need to be afraid."

Emma backed further away. "I'm not..." She cut off her next words. Tell them she wasn't afraid and then what? What reason did she have for not learning to ride this very day? "Did you ride the horse then?" Her voice snapped out like an accusation.

Edward's brow creased. "Uh, yes. She needed exercise.

I took her for a run yesterday."

"Let me see."

He looked confused.

"Let me see you ride the horse."

"I, uh, I can't. Not with this saddle. It's a sidesaddle as you can see."

"An' you can't ride in a sidesaddle?"

Edward shifted his weight. His eyes turned to Tall Joe.

"It wouldn't be right," Tall Joe explained, speaking slowly, as though she were a very young child who had difficulty understanding the way of the world. "Sidesaddles are for ladies only. Edward can't ride sidesaddle any more than you can ride with a man's saddle."

Well, and no one ever called her a lady before! That was the first thought that flitted through Emma's mind. Aloud, she said, "An' if a lady wants to use a proper saddle, what then?"

The two men exchanged glances. Then Edward looked her way, shaking his head ever so slightly.

Tall Joe's lips set in a hard line. He put his head back, rubbed a hand over his full beard, and glared down at her, eyebrows raised. "Such a thing is unacceptable, Emma. Ladies must ride sidesaddle. It's one of society's rules. With your long skirts and all, it really is the only way. You should know that."

"An' what would happen to society if a girl used the wrong saddle?"

"Well it...I...it simply isn't done." Tall Joe bristled.

Edward rubbed the horse's mane. Tall Joe glared at Emma over his dark beard. Emma shifted her weight to her left leg.

The stranger appeared out of nowhere, her voice clear and sharp behind Emma.

DAYLE CAMPBELL GAETZ

"If you ask me, it's a stupid rule! Can't you see how much safer it is to ride *astride* a horse, especially on rugged mountain passes and trails no wider than a horse's hoof cut into the side of a sheer rock face? And who makes up these silly rules anyway? It's always us girls who aren't allowed to do this or that or anything half adventurous, and no one gives us any say in the matter!"

Emma spun around. The girl who stood behind her, only a few feet away, was about Emma's own age. Not so tall as Emma, she had a straight, narrow nose, round, dark eyes and a small pink mouth. A fringe of brown hair peeked from the front of the warm cap she had pulled down over her ears. Her clothes were simple but warm-looking and well made. The wool skirt fell in soft folds to cover the tops of her boots.

Emma recognized her immediately. This was the girl she had seen a few days ago, when they brought the horse to town tied behind the cart. But where had she come from? Emma didn't trust her, sneaking up from behind like some gonoph, ready to rob them of all they owned.

Before anyone could think of an answer to the girl's outspoken words, the horse gave a toss of its mane. It snorted softly, dark eyes fixed on the newcomer. Edward let go of the reins, and the horse trotted as close to the girl as possible, reaching its long neck over the fence toward her. The girl's face lit up, and her cheeks flushed pink, which made her look quite pretty, Emma noticed.

"Nugget!" the stranger whispered. She reached up to stroke the horse's nose, then scrambled onto the middle rail and pressed her face against its wide forehead. "Oh, Nugget, I've missed you so much!" When the girl pulled back, her eyes were filled with tears.

Finally Emma found her voice. "Who are you?" Her words hung harsh and loud in the chill air, sounding rude even if she had not meant them to be.

The girl glanced sideways at Emma. "My name is Katherine Harris, and this beautiful horse used to be mine.".

Emma cringed at the sound of that voice, so very proper, exactly the way Emma's mother had tried to teach her to speak. But Emma had grown up with the people of the streets, living in the netherskens and toiling in the textile mills of Manchester. That was where she learned most of her speech patterns. This Katherine sounded exactly like any rich lady in England, a lady who would march past a poor girl selling apples on the street, holding her delicate nose in the air with a lace handkerchief clamped over it. 'Cause you never knew, that stench of poverty might seep right into her little brain and make her ill, poor fragile little creature that she was.

The girl's steady gaze did not waver. Emma wished she would go away so they would never need to talk. If Emma opened her mouth again, this Katherine would know she was from a lower class. She would turn her nose up and think herself so much better.

"Pleased to meet you, Miss Harris." Tall Joe stepped forward to shake the girl's hand. "I'm Joseph Bentley, this is Emma Curtis, and that's Edward, who works at Beckley Farm here."

Edward mumbled something that sounded polite, and Emma nodded in the girl's direction. Katherine Harris, she thought, an' she must be the mayor's daughter. Thomas Harris, who bought this horse, won his race at Beacon Hill on it and sold it so the poor horse wouldn't be squashed to a pile of bones under his great weight.

Odd the man didn't give the horse to his own daughter, since she seemed that fond of it. And this Katherine was so small the horse would never so much as know she was there. The girl did not take after her great lump of a father and that's for certain-sure. Emma waited impatiently for the girl to be done with patting the horse and go off about her business.

"Do you want to ride her?" Edward asked.

Emma glared at him.

Edward caught her quick look of surprise, laced with anger, and had the good sense to look uneasy. "Well, but you don't want to Emma, and maybe Miss Harris here can show you how it's done."

Emma's face burned. She did not need some fancy city toff showing her what to do. She turned to Tall Joe for help.

"Excellent idea!" Tall Joe beamed. "Emma seems a little nervous with us two males hanging about. Could be she'll feel more comfortable with another female around." His eyes turned toward Emma, noted her angry scowl, and skittered away. "You did say you'd like someone to show you how to ride the horse, Emma."

"Well, if you don't mind." Katherine looked at Emma as if asking for permission. As if she really would refuse if Emma objected. Emma saw the excitement on the girl's face. This Katherine Harris could scarcely wait to climb over the fence and up onto the horse.

Emma shrugged. What did she care?

Could be this was a good thing, Emma told herself a few minutes later. With this Katherine riding the horse, they forgot all about her. She stepped onto the bottom rail and watched Katherine trot the horse expertly about in circles. The horse broke into a canter, and Katherine rode smoothly with it, her back straight, looking quite elegant, as if balancing up there with the horse bouncing and charging about was as simple as sitting on a parlour chair.

That's when the rain began. Not slowly, but with great huge globs that fell hard and fast from the low-hanging clouds and spattered over Emma's head and shoulders. She shivered, but the others didn't seem to notice the rain.

When at last Katherine brought the horse to a stop, she laughed out loud. She looked very pretty with her flushed face and bright smile. Tall Joe and Edward gathered close. They looked to have forgotten the girl's earlier words that left them speechless. They looked to have forgotten Emma too.

Emma waited for them to come over to her, or look at her, or remember she was standing here, getting soaked by rain that poured down in cold hard sheets. But no one so much as glanced her way. Those three chattered on about horses and riding and what a beautiful mare Nugget was and how well Katherine handled her and how gracefully the two of them, horse and rider, moved together.

Well, and Emma supposed Tall Joe was happy now and Edward too. They didn't need her. Watching them, she became more and more aware of the ache in her right hip and knee. It hurt so bad in this rain she would never be able to hide her limp when she walked home.

Quietly, so as not to call attention to herself – not that they would take any notice of her anyway – Emma stepped down from the fence rail. But as soon as she put weight on her right leg, it gave out. Pain shot from her hip right down to her ankle. She grabbed the fence to keep from falling.

Hoping no one had noticed, Emma glanced from Tall Joe to Edward. Seemed like they had forgotten all about her. Seemed like that Katherine Harris suited them much better than her. And that was good, Emma told herself, forcing her lips into a weak smile. Now she was free to do as she pleased. She turned and walked away, taking small steps, trying not to limp.

She had no idea what to do with the rest of this gloomy afternoon.

Katherine and Emma

Who Is She? – The mysterious female who...rejoices in her ability to ride in public astraddle of a horse, is reported to have been seen again on the Esquimalt Road yesterday... Accompanying the mysterious female was another feminine, who seemed to possess a little more modesty...and sported a lady's black riding habit.

– *The British Colonist*, April 25, 1862

7

Katherine could scarcely believe her luck. She was, right this very minute, riding her wonderful horse again. But not for long. Soon she would have to stop because that girl, that Emma, would surely want to have her turn even if she looked as though she'd rather be anywhere in the world but here. Once more around and she would stop. Or twice. Yes, two more times around the muddy little paddock and then she really would have to quit. Katherine could tell by the way the horse moved beneath her that Nugget yearned to stretch her long legs into a gallop and run until her muscles grew tired and her breathing became labored.

In the end, Katherine couldn't help herself. She urged her horse into a gentle canter and rode several more times around the paddock before pulling up beside the man and boy, laughing because she felt so good and had enjoyed the ride so much. "That was marvelous!" she told them. "Nugget is such a perfect horse!"

"She is indeed," Bentley agreed, "and you're a very accomplished young horsewoman. May I ask where you learned to ride?"

"Oh, at home in England before we moved to the colonies. My father insisted I take lessons." Katherine could not bring herself to dismount, partly because this might be the last time she ever rode Nugget but mostly because she didn't want to risk falling on her face in the mud with these three strangers looking on. "But since we started working a farm over in British Columbia, I didn't ride – until I got Nugget, of course."

"Why did you sell your horse?" It was the young man who spoke. Edward.

Katherine hesitated, too proud to admit how poor they had become since leaving England. "I had to sell her because we didn't need two horses on the farm."

Mr. Bentley scratched his beard and gazed up at Katherine, his eyes narrowed in suspicion. "You're certain of that?" he demanded. "You owned this very same horse?"

"Of course I'm certain." Katherine tried to keep the anger from her voice. "Do you think I don't know my own horse? Wednesday afternoon I saw her tied behind a cart, so I followed until I knew where she was being taken." Katherine glared down at the man, but Bentley didn't appear to notice. He raised both hands to help her from the saddle.

She ignored his offer, determined to dismount on her own. Katherine had practiced her dismount from a side-saddle many times since that embarrassing tumble in Hope. For the most part, she managed not to fall, even though the process was never easy. With her left foot secure in the stirrup, she released her leg from the curved pommel that held it in place. Then she freed her right leg, curled around the upper pommel. She twisted her body around, gripped the top pommel, slightly off-centred near the top of the saddle, and finally pulled her foot from the stirrup. Nugget stood perfectly still as Katherine eased herself down. The muddy ground was slippery beneath her feet, but the closeness of her horse steadied her.

Katherine turned to Mr. Bentley, still angry that he doubted her. But the man only smiled, not really seeing her at all. He lifted himself up on his toes and down again. "I had a feeling she would make a good horse for a young lady. That's why I bought her for Emma here." He turned around.

His shoulders sagged when he saw the empty fence. He looked back at Katherine. Almost hidden in his dark beard, his mouth was set in a grim line.

Katherine was not surprised by Emma's disappearance. She wondered why this Joseph Bentley chose to buy Nugget for the girl at all. "Did Emma say she wanted Nugget?"

Mr. Bentley's dark eyebrows raised. He shook his head. "No."

"Then she only mentioned she would like a horse of her own?"

His eyebrows lowered, he crossed his arms. "She didn't say that either."

"I see." Katherine nodded as if she understood perfectly, but in truth she had a lot more questions. She wondered whether this girl, Emma Curtis, was a friend of Mr. Bentley or perhaps his niece? The girl was tall and had a look about her that made it difficult to estimate her age, but Katherine guessed she must be several years older than herself. There was a worldliness about Emma; those big, dark eyes of hers held a knowledge and maturity that came only with time and experience.

Katherine opened her mouth, another question formed and ready to spill out: *Why would you purchase a horse for a girl who, by the look of her, doesn't even like them?*

But something in the way Joseph Bentley looked down at her, in the way his black eyes flashed with a promise of anger, warned her to keep quiet. If this man were anything like her father, he would not welcome being interrogated by a young girl such as herself, especially after the way she went on about riding sidesaddle. So she closed her mouth, cut off the question.

The "Wh..." had escaped though, before she could stop it. Katherine covered her mouth, pretended to cough. She looked at the young man and was surprised to see him suppress a smile. He winked at her, as if he knew exactly what she was thinking.

This Edward had a way about him that made Katherine feel she could trust him on first sight. His friendly face was almost perfectly round and so open and amiable she wondered if he had ever been angry a minute in his life. And the way he moved reminded Katherine of that half-grown bear cub in her garden, loping along on legs that had grown so long its body needed time to catch up. In spite of his height and broad shoulders, she was certain he was younger than her brother. Katherine expected Edward was one of those people everyone liked, whether they were young, old, or in between.

"Uh, sir?" Edward ventured. "Could I speak to you for a moment, sir?"

When Bentley turned his way, Edward nodded toward the open stable door.

"Right, good idea," Bentley murmured. "It's time we all got out of this rain, in any event." He looked at Katherine as if wondering what to do with her.

"If you don't mind, Mr. Bentley, might I bring Nugget into the stable and give her a rub down?"

The man's eyebrows rose and a crease appeared between them. "But are you certain you want to? Edward is here to take care of such dirty tasks."

Katherine nodded. "Yes, sir, I really would like to."

She followed the men into the barn and led Nugget to the stall Edward pointed out. While she set to work removing Nugget's saddle, the men moved farther away. She could hear their murmured conversation as she rubbed Nugget's coat with the curry comb, but was far more interested in her horse than anything they had to say. "Did you miss me, Nugget? You must be lonely with no one to ride you and take proper care of you."

She brushed away dirt and bits of mud loosened by the comb. "I don't know what's wrong with that girl, Emma. She looks so cross I suspect she must be spoiled to the core. She's likely used to being handed everything she ever wants." Katherine paused for a moment, thinking about Emma. "But even so, underneath it all she was frightened of something." Katherine reached up to brush the thick, soft hair of Nugget's neck. "Do you think it could be you she's afraid of?"

Katherine found it almost impossible to imagine that anyone would be afraid of Nugget, yet that was what she had seen written on the girl's face. The first moment Emma glanced her way, Katherine had seen the fear, even though Emma tried to disguise it as anger. Her large, unusually dark eyes narrowed and her eyebrows pulled together above them, but her wide mouth, even though she tried to hold it in a firm line, trembled around its edges. Katherine understood exactly how it felt to be quaking with fear on the inside while acting angry and unafraid for the world to see.

"I'm so glad I found you, Nugget," Katherine whispered, brushing Nugget's neck. "Can you ever forgive me for selling you? I didn't want to, you know that, don't you?"

Someone coughed, and Katherine glanced over her shoulder to see Mr. Bentley and Edward leaning on the gate to Nugget's stall as if unwilling to interrupt. She stopped brushing and turned to face them.

"Miss Harris, I would very much appreciate it if you would grant me a few minutes of your time."

Mr. Bentley was so terribly formal and polite Katherine had no idea how to deal with him. He treated her like a grown-up woman and a lady at that. Not at all the way her father acted, as if she were a young, rather foolish child. Mr. Bentley's manner made her feel awkward and uncomfortable. She felt like an impostor soon to be discovered through a careless word or a silly blunder. And that made her afraid to open her mouth.

She glanced at Edward, who nodded encouragement. "I'll finish grooming Nugget for you," he offered.

Katherine smiled, pleased to hear him use the name she had given her horse. She followed Mr. Bentley, who walked a short distance before stopping near the stall of a stocky old grey horse, who blinked up at Katherine with moist, tired eyes.

"Well, Miss Harris," Bentley said, "it seems young Edward thinks you would be the perfect person to teach Miss Curtis to ride."

Katherine studied Mr. Bentley. The man really was incredibly tall, with those long legs of his. And the way he scowled over his beard from so high above made Katherine curious to know why he cared so much about Emma

Curtis. Why should he concern himself if Emma learned to ride a horse or not?

You mustn't stick your nose into places it does not belong. Her mother's words slid into her mind just in time. Katherine bit her lip to keep from asking a question best left alone.

"You see," Bentley continued, "I had asked Edward to teach Miss Curtis. It seemed to be a good plan and Edward agreed to do it, but he is now convinced Emma is cross at the both of us because we made our plans without ever asking what she wanted." He seemed confused by this thought, shaking his head as if it made no sense at all.

Katherine nodded. "Of course she would be angry then."

Apparently this was not the correct response, because Mr. Bentley's eyebrows pulled together. Head bent back, he rubbed a hand over his beard and scowled down at her. "I shall pay you, naturally, for your time."

This came as such a surprise Katherine almost laughed out loud. Mr. Bentley would pay her to spend time with the horse she loved? But the money would be useful; she could use it to help pay her board. Even so, she felt uncomfortable accepting the task. "I shall agree to teach her, but only if Emma wants me to," she said.

Bentley sighed. His dark eyes narrowed in frustration.

"May I say something?"

They both jumped. Bentley gave a curt nod in Edward's direction.

"All right then sir, here's what I think." Edward spoke slowly, feeling for the correct words. "Instead of paying me to do it, you ought to pay Katherine here to exercise Nugget and groom her too. Do that, and before much time goes by Emma will happen along on her own."

Bentley looked uncertain, but Katherine jumped at the opportunity. "I would love it!" she said. "I could ride Nugget every day after school! And if Emma asks me to teach her, I'll help her learn to ride."

Katherine could scarcely imagine why she deserved so much good luck in one day. Unable to keep a smile from spreading across her face, she turned from Edward's pleased expression to Mr. Bentley's grim one. The man looked baffled, as if the very idea that others might see the world differently from himself had never once occurred to him.

"I fail to understand why she would," he growled. "You don't know Emma, she is a very stubborn young lady and won't stand for anyone telling her what to do."

"Sorry, sir, but I disagree. I know Emma, perhaps better than anyone," Edward pointed out. "I watched her the day she stepped off the steamer. Our Emma held her head so proud!" He smiled, remembering. "So, sir, I do understand how Emma feels. That girl needs to make up her own mind whether to come here or not. You're correct that she will never be forced into anything, but Emma's own curiosity will bring her here. I'm certain of it."

Bentley glanced from Edward to Katherine, his face glum, as if he would prefer to be the one who knew Emma best.

"It's easier for us to know how Emma feels," Katherine explained, in an attempt to make him feel better, "not being quite so old as yourself."

At this, Bentley's eyebrows lowered and his mouth pulled into a rigid line. The man looked so disgruntled Katherine decided it was time to stop talking altogether.

Everything she said turned out to be wrong. She turned to Edward in a silent appeal, but he only shook his head and kept his own mouth shut tight.

The silence lengthened. Soaked to the skin, Katherine shivered in a cool breeze that blew through the wide barn door. She watched Mr. Bentley, certain he would change his mind about letting her ride Nugget after the way she insulted him, even if she hadn't meant to.

He stood very still, staring out the door, his right fist pressed against his beard, right elbow cupped in his left hand. The man most definitely did not look happy. More, he seemed stunned, as though he had just been delivered some very bad news. Did the man never look in a mirror? Did he really think himself young?

Edward's hands hung loosely in his pockets. He appeared to have developed an uncommon interest in the rafters above their heads. Or perhaps he was searching for a quick means of escape.

At last Bentley grunted, in the same way George always did when he couldn't think what to say. Katherine lifted her chin, bracing herself for bad news.

The man dropped his hand and turned to Katherine, his face so stern and unforgiving that she cringed. "All right then," he snapped, "we'll try it your way." He strode from the barn without a backward glance.

The following day at school, Katherine could scarcely concentrate. She sat at her little wooden desk and attempted to keep her mind on her work, but the lessons here were not nearly so challenging as in England. With over fifty pupils of all ages and abilities, Mr. Brett had a difficult time teaching everyone and had no time to prepare special lessons for Katherine.

The final bell had not finished ringing when Katherine grabbed her books and ran out the door. Hunched over the little bundle, she scurried through driving rain and splashed over thick, slippery mud so deep in places she was forced to take slow steps, pulling her boots one after the other out of the muck. She reached Mrs. Morris' cottage near the north shore of James Bay and walked around to the back door, thick mud clinging to her boots. On the covered porch she removed her boots and left them there. She stepped inside.

As usual, Mrs. Morris wasn't at home. Katherine hurried upstairs to change her clothes. Cook was nowhere to be seen either, so as Katherine passed back through the kitchen, she sliced herself a thick piece of freshly baked bread, slathered it with butter, and dashed out the back door before Mrs. Morris could come home and insist Katherine stay inside in such weather or catch her death of cold. Not that Mrs. Morris cared about Katherine's health. The older woman might have promised Katherine's mother to *care for her as if she were my own daughter,* but the minute Mother left, Mrs. Morris scarcely paid any attention to her at all. And that suited Katherine just fine.

A dark and threatening sky hung low over bare oak trees, but the rain slowed to a drizzle as Katherine made her way across James Bay Bridge, past the government office buildings everyone called the Birdcages, past the big white house where Governor Douglas and his family lived, and on to Beckley Farm. No one was around as she hurried into the barn.

"Nugget!" she called softly, and her horse answered with a welcoming snort. Katherine was pleased to see Nugget already bridled and saddled. This gave her extra time to ride on dreary afternoons when darkness closed in earlier and earlier. She led Nugget from the barn, used a large round of cedar tree as a block to climb onto the sidesaddle, and set off toward Beacon Hill.

Again, on Tuesday, Nugget was bridled and saddled, and Katherine suspected it was Edward who did this for her, even though she had not seen him again. This afternoon she waited for some time, trotting the horse around the yard in case Emma might show up. But no one was around, no one to ask, and the trail beckoned her away.

Katherine was back and grooming the horse when Edward stopped by.

"Tomorrow is my half day off," he mentioned casually. "And Emma's too."

"Yes? Have you figured a way to get her over here?"

He removed his hat and ran his fingers through his hair. "I'm working on it."

8

Wednesday morning, halfway to noon, and Emma had not one plan for her afternoon off. On hands and knees, she scrubbed the kitchen floor, pouring every scrap of energy into her work as if she could scrub right through to the earth below. She tried to keep thoughts from filling her head, those thoughts that kept coming back when she never did want them in the first place.

It didn't work. "All this time to myself with no one pesterin' me," she mumbled, "an' I should be happy."

Last Sunday after leaving Beckley Farm, Emma had moved along the trail as fast as she could, which was not fast at all, limping her way home, afraid Tall Joe would catch up and insist she return to Beckley Farm in spite of the drenching rain.

But no one came after her. Neither one of them so much as turned his head and took notice when she left. Too busy talking to that Katherine, they were, thinking she was so perfect just because she could climb on a horse and not go tumbling down to the mud. And her sitting there so straight in that wretched sidesaddle, smiling like the blooming Queen of England, so proud of herself and all.

"So, Emma, I suppose you're going over to the farm

to visit your horse this afternoon?" Mrs. Douglas asked when the two of them sat in the big, warm kitchen eating lunch.

To hide her surprise, Emma took a huge bite of bread, soft and warm from the oven. And how did Mrs. Douglas know about the horse?

As if Emma had asked the question out loud, Mrs. Douglas said, "Your father told me he was buying you a horse. He was so excited he couldn't stop smiling!"

When Emma didn't answer but picked up her teacup instead, Mrs. Douglas continued in her soft-spoken way. "The sternwheelers can't take you beyond Fort Yale, Emma, and in spring with snow melting and the Fraser running high, any boat will be lucky to get past Fort Hope. After that you'll face steep and rugged mountain trails. You will need to ride well by spring."

"Not if I don't go."

Even if she refused to look at her employer, Emma could feel Mrs. Douglas' surprise and so busied herself pouring a second cup of tea for each of them. Mrs. Douglas did not ask any questions, and Emma was grateful because she didn't feel like talking. She needed to get out of this house. Now.

Oh, but not without eating first. Emma had gone too many years with hunger gnawing at her belly to turn down good food, so she set about finishing her meal quickly.

The day was mild with high-up clouds and not one bit of wind as Emma started down the front walk. No one could tell if her leg hurt or not, because the pain was almost gone and she walked with scarcely a limp. Of their own accord, as if they belonged to someone else, her feet turned toward Beckley Farm, but Emma soon straightened them out and headed for the bridge instead. She had no other plans but to take a walk, to be on her own where she could think things through. A horse changed everything. She would tell Tall Joe soon, the next time she saw him, that she had changed her mind.

She was happy enough in the Douglas home. Mrs. Douglas was the kindest, warmest woman in the world and couldn't help herself, she was a mother to everyone who needed her, especially Emma. So Emma could stay right here in Victoria, where she was safe, and not go running off to start a farm with Tall Joe and that cousin of his, Ned Turner.

And if she didn't go she would never need to ride a horse at all. Not ever.

Emma stopped at the James Bay bridge. She gazed down at the ring on her left hand, the ring her mam gave Emma before she up and died. Emma ran her fingertips over the warmth of the oval stone, set in gold filigree. She turned her hand this way and that, admiring how the white stone shimmered green and purple and blue even in today's dull light. She must have been daft when she tried to sell it. Daft and that angry at her mother for giving up and dying on her.

Emma dropped her hand to her side and started walking again. "I miss you, Mama," she whispered. She tried to think what her mother would suggest in these circumstances.

Emma strolled onto the bridge, remembering the plans she had made when she first arrived here. All she wanted back then was to leave Vancouver's Island and make her way across the strait to that other colony, the one she heard talk of back in England. "British Columbia," she whispered. Even now the sound of it made beautiful pictures in her mind. In British Columbia the land sparkled with gold wherever the sun shone upon it. She would travel there and never leave until she got rich. That was what she had thought back then, foolish girl that she was.

Once here she saw all those men on the streets of Victoria and her dream ended. Dirty, ragged men they were, who had spent every penny they owned to get to the Cariboo and strike it rich. Now they hung about with not enough money to buy their passage home. Some few of those men had snatched up brideship girls as they were paraded down the street on their first day off the ship. Emma felt her anger rise, recalling that grimy man who dared approach her. And she scared him off with a look.

She was lucky to have found a safe place to live.

Deep in thought, Emma didn't take notice of footsteps thudding up behind her on the wooden bridge. She jumped and spun around when a hand touched her shoulder.

"Edward!" Emma was so pleased to see him standing there, his smile as familiar and friendly as always, that she almost smiled in return, almost forgot she was that angry at him. She remembered just in time and started walking again, faster than before, even if it did make her leg hurt more. Edward fell into step beside her.

"An' what brings you here?" she demanded. "I thought you'd be off riding that horse you think's so marvelous!"

Edward shrugged. "Don't need to. Katherine's taking care of Nugget for you. She comes to the farm every day after school."

Emma almost stumbled but caught herself in time. "Katherine? An' why would she want to do that?"

"Because she loves the horse, Emma. Nugget used to be hers, as you know, and Katherine misses riding her. Your father is paying her to exercise the horse every day after school and groom her too. But I expect she would do it for nothing."

As if that girl needs to be paid, thought Emma, surprised Katherine would accept payment, being an upper class young lady and all, who thought folks who earned their own way in this world were beneath them. "Thought you were doing that."

Edward removed his hat. His curls tumbled about his face as he scratched his head, thinking. "Mr. Bentley asked me, and I tried it too, but there's not so much time left over with chores on the farm and all."

Emma didn't want to think about Katherine any more. "What's there to do on a dull day like this?" she asked, half-hoping Edward would suggest something. Maybe they could go walking together, or visit that family of his she'd never met. Just last spring Edward's father had died of the smallpox, Emma knew that much, and Edward worked hard to help his mother support the family.

"I'll be off to visit my mother and the children then," Edward said. "I want to get back in time to help Katherine when she arrives after school."

He strode off, and Emma glared after him, her fists clenched tight with anger. And what a foolish girl you are, Emma Curtis, forgetting to be cross at Edward. She should never have talked to him at all. And him in a great hurry to get back to the farm and that Katherine he liked so much.

Well, and why should she care what Edward did? Emma continued on her way, wandering aimlessly along the streets of Victoria. What should she do with the rest of this day? She stopped outside a market where a wooden box near the door was filled to overflowing with apples so round and red they made her mouth water just looking at them. Emma realized, with pride, that she had more than enough money to purchase one for herself. She hurried inside, asked for the biggest, reddest apple and paid for it with pennies from her pocket. At the door, she stopped and turned back. "Could I have another one, please?" she asked the storekeeper.

And it's time you stopped acting such a great fool, Emma told herself as she walked back toward the bridge, munching on her apple. If she could face up to that great, fat lout of a bailiff back in Manchester, if she could make her way alone through the English countryside, if she could travel half across the world in the hold of a damp and stinking steamship, then she would not let one dumb animal defeat her.

She had this one chance to better herself in life, and wouldn't she be daft to toss it away without even trying? Fact was, if she could not ride, she could not go where she wanted. Not ever. As good as Mrs. Douglas was to her, Emma didn't want to spend her whole entire life as a maidservant.

Right now was the perfect time. With Tall Joe off somewhere and not taking the time to pester her, with Edward visiting his mother, and that Katherine sitting in her fancy school learning who knew what, no one would be there to watch if Emma's hand shook or she backed suddenly away without meaning to. She would face up to that animal and teach herself not to be afraid.

"An' that's for certain-sure," she whispered.

No one was about as Emma crossed the Beckley Farm

property and slipped into the barn. She paused there, gazing into corners to be sure no one lurked in the shadows. The sharp smell of hay and horse dung shot straight up through her nose and stung her eyes but wasn't nearly so horrible as those streets of Manchester where the stench sometimes got so strong it made her stomach turn over. No, this smell was not so bad at all.

With her eyes adjusted to the dim light, Emma started down the centre of the barn. Two horses watched her from their stalls, two big, heavy brutes with thick brown manes and broad white stripes down their wide faces. Those fierce dark eyes of theirs followed her every move as Emma edged past them, staying as far away as she could, certain the horses would reach their long necks out and grab her with their great yellow teeth if given half a chance. Close to her now was a third horse, one Emma had not noticed at first. It was pale grey and much smaller than the others. This one's head hung low. It took little interest in Emma.

She stopped and studied the horse more closely. It looked sad, or afraid, she wasn't sure which. "You poor thing," Emma said, "you look as happy to be here as I am." The horse didn't look up. "An' I must be daft. Standin' here talkin' to a dumb animal like it knows what I'm sayin'." Emma started walking again.

The fourth horse was not so heavyset as those big brown beasts but far taller and more graceful than the grey one. Its rich brown face and long neck were slender and refined. Emma stood very still and watched this horse. The animal watched her too with those wide brown eyes. Emma took a step closer, and the horse lifted its head, giving its long black mane a shake. Emma's breath caught in her throat. She forced herself not to turn and run.

She swallowed, breathed in once, then out, then in again. She gathered her courage and began to speak, softly, just the way Edward had talked to the horse. "I'm come to make friends," she said. "Just so you know, I'm not scared of you, if that's what you're thinkin'."

The horse snorted. Emma jumped back.

"Well, an' could be I am just a small bit scared, since you mention it, but you are a great huge beast, whether you know it or not with those heavy hoofs of yours that knock people down in the street and trample them into the mud."

Emma took a step closer, a very small one. Then another. With each step the horse seemed to grow that much bigger. She kept talking, trying to reassure herself as much as the horse. "An' even if I am scared, I won't ever let that stop me. If a horse is the only way to get me where I want to go, then I can do it, I can learn to ride you and not be afraid. An' that's for certain-sure."

She stood for a moment then, staring up at the horse as if she expected a reply, but the horse only looked back at her. "I brought you an apple," Emma said, holding it up. "If you want to know, you're a lucky horse to have an apple to eat. I never so much as tasted one when I grew up in England. I sold them though, on the streets of Manchester, to rich ladies like your Miss Katherine Harris."

She took a few more tentative steps forward and suddenly realized with one small step more she would be close enough to reach out and touch the horse, if she wanted. Which she didn't. Where she stood now seemed entirely too close already. The horse chose that moment to snort and lift its head high. It glared down its long face at Emma, its nostrils flared. As quickly, it lowered its head and pushed its nose toward Emma. She gasped and jumped back. Her heart pounded against her ribs.

"It's the apple she wants," said a voice behind her. "Nugget won't hurt you."

It was that Katherine Harris, with her fancy way of talking and all. Emma was deeply embarrassed to be caught this way when she only wanted to spend time getting to know the horse with no one here to make fun of her. She whirled around, words already formed on her tongue. *An' who do you think you are, I'd like to know? Sneakin' up on a body like you was some gonoph ready to rob a girl of all she owns?*

But even as she opened her mouth, Emma reminded herself to speak the way her mother taught her. She would not have this girl thinking she was better than her just because of the way she spoke. "I am not afraid of the horse," she said, her voice tight and angry. "I was only startled when it moved so quickly. I am not used to horses. Neither am I used to people creeping up from behind." She wondered how long Katherine had been standing there watching.

Katherine's forehead crinkled. "Emma, I only just now came through the door and saw you jump back. I thought you looked nervous of Nugget, but you needn't be, she's very gentle."

"Why do you call it Nugget?"

Katherine stiffened. She hesitated for a moment, then said, "It was because of a gold nugget that I was able to purchase a horse in the first place."

Emma couldn't imagine how this could be. She knew for a fact Tall Joe bought the horse from Mayor Harris.

And hadn't she seen the mayor win a race on this very horse? This Katherine Harris said the horse was once hers, so she must be related to the mayor. Then what was this about a gold nugget?

"I think I'll change its name," Emma said, more to annoy Katherine than for any other reason. Even as she said it she had no idea of a name, except that it should have something to do with freedom. It came to her in a flash. "I think I'll call it Liberty."

Katherine pressed her lips together. After a moment, she opened her mouth to speak but glanced over at the horse and seemed almost to bite her tongue. "Whatever name you call her," she said at last, "the horse needs to be exercised and Mr. Bentley asked me to do that, so I'll get busy now if you don't mind."

Katherine stomped away, leaving Emma to shiver in a cold draft that trickled through the open doorway. And what should she do now? Turn around, walk out the door, and not ever come back? Something told her this Katherine would not be bothered at all if she left. That girl would be happy enough to see the backside of Emma Curtis and have the horse all to herself. And she'd have Tall Joe and Edward to herself at the same time.

Emma heard a clink and a thud and there was Katherine back again, carrying that awful saddle. "Edward usually does this for me," she said. "But I'm here a bit early today." She placed the saddle over the stall gate and stood back to study it. "I'm tempted to put a man's saddle on her instead of this sidesaddle."

Emma felt a little burst of hope.

"But if Mr. Bentley found out he'd likely be so shocked he would never let me ride Nugget again."

Liberty, Emma wanted to say.

Katherine looked down at Emma's hand. "Are you planning to give that to her or did you bring it for yourself?"

Emma had almost forgotten the apple. "I brought it for the horse."

"That's what I figured. So I got you a knife from the tack room."

"Thank you," Emma said stiffly. She waited for Katherine to walk away, then started slicing the apple the same way Tall Joe had done at Craigflower Farm. Her fingers felt clumsy and her hands shook a little, she was that nervous. And how was she supposed to get close to the horse with that wretched Katherine watching her every move, she'd like to know? She should never have come here at all.

And just look at that foolish girl, standing inside the stall stroking the horse's mane. *She's waiting for me,* thought Emma, *standing there waiting to watch me make a great, huge fool of myself so she can tell Edward and those two can have a good laugh after I drop the apple and run. Well, and I'll show her Emma Curtis isn't so scared after all.*

Slowly, one step at a time, Emma moved closer to the stall.

Katherine looked up. "Just hold it out to her. She'll take it gently; she doesn't enjoy the taste of fingers."

Emma held out an apple slice, clutching the very tip between her thumb and forefinger. She stretched her arm. The horse stretched its neck. Warm, moist breath drizzled over Emma's hand. She pulled back. But only a little. She glanced at Katherine and away. She had to do this. Had to. Emma stopped breathing. She watched her own hand, the apple slice. Saw those great, grinding teeth. Shut her eyes.

"There," Katherine said, "that wasn't so difficult was it?"

Emma blinked. The horse munched down the apple slice and looked for more. She did it! Emma handed over another piece, and another, until all the apple was gone.

Katherine smiled at her, and Emma looked back without scowling. Maybe this Katherine wasn't so bad after all, at least with no one around to show off for. And she didn't look down her nose to remind Emma she was a worthless little servant girl.

Katherine placed a blanket over the horse's back and then the saddle. When she bent under its stomach to cinch the saddle, Emma eyed those heavy hoofs and waited for the horse to kick. But that huge beast stood perfectly still.

Katherine held the reins close under the horse's chin and looked up. "Now," she said, "if you want, you can stroke her on the face. She'd like that. Don't worry, she won't hurt you. She only wants to thank you for bringing her an apple."

Well, and if that wasn't a foolish thing to say Emma didn't know what was. As if an animal had sense enough to thank a person for such a gift. Emma almost laughed at the very thought, but the expression on Katherine's face was so serious and the horse was standing so close, her laughter died before it began.

Of course the horse wouldn't bite her, Emma understood that. Of course there was no harm in touching it, she actually wanted to now. At the same time something held her back, some dreadful, senseless fear she did not understand and wished would go away. But it enveloped her nevertheless. Her heart beat too fast, her palms felt wet, and her breath lodged in her throat.

"It's all right, if you don't want to." Katherine unlatched the gate and started to push it open. "You fed her the apple at least."

"No." Emma's voice trembled. She took a breath and tried again, struggling to get the words out before they choked her. "No, I want to. Really. I just...I have never done it before."

Emma had never been so close to a horse before and the fear inside her was almost too much to bear. The first lesson she remembered as a tiny girl reaching up to clutch her mother's hand was to always stay clear of those great hoofs that would squash you into the muck if you didn't watch out.

Katherine tapped the toe of her boot against the straw. When Emma simply stood there, staring straight ahead, she placed her own hand on Nugget's face, just below the horse's eyes. "Simply touch her, gently, like this. It's very soothing for Nugget."

Emma had to do it now, either that or look the complete fool. Right now, while the girl's hand was still there and before she lost all patience. Emma lifted her left hand, palm toward the horse, fingers slightly apart. Closer, just inches away now. She could do it, she would do it. Yes. The broad face felt warm beneath her fingers, not so frightening at all.

"That's good. Now move your hand gently down toward her nostrils."

She did. Partway down, a matter of inches. She glanced at Katherine, proud of her accomplishment. But

Katherine didn't look up; she only stared at Emma's left hand, at the opal ring.

Emma yanked her hand away. Pressing it close against her side, she stepped out of the way while Katherine led the horse from the stall. Katherine paused there, frowning up at Emma, her lips pressed tight together as if holding back from asking a question.

And if she asks me to try riding, what excuse do I have? "I must be going," she said. "It's getting late." She stepped back to let them pass.

Emma watched them from behind, the small girl and the big horse, silhouetted against the wide open door. Katherine climbed onto a block of wood and from there pulled herself into the saddle. Emma kept herself hidden in the dark shadows of the barn, watching until Katherine disappeared around a bend in the road. Then she turned to go. She couldn't imagine why it should matter what Katherine Harris thought of her, but it did.

At the edge of Beckley Farm, Emma met up with Edward. "You're too late," she told him. "That Katherine has saddled the horse and gone off." She watched his face for a sign he was disappointed, but he only smiled as if he was happy to see her.

"Good then, that saves me the trouble. And I can walk with you. If you don't mind, that is."

Emma didn't mind. Not at all. She was that glad of his company. "Suit yourself, Edward," she shrugged. "I can't stop you from walking where you want to go, this being a public road and all."

Edward laughed.

And what was so funny, she'd like to know?

As they walked, Emma considered telling Edward

about her triumph. She had fed a whole, entire apple to the horse and not even backed away from touching it, right there between the eyes. But she realized that to Edward this would seem a small enough victory. Scarcely worth mentioning. She would wait and hope to surprise him one day when she was up and sitting in the saddle. Both him and Tall Joe, wouldn't they just fall over with surprise?

A thought came to her then. An idea she would put aside for now and consider more deeply when she had the time. Maybe that Katherine girl would teach her how to ride the horse when no one else was about.

9

At the track below Beacon Hill, Katherine tapped Nugget with her riding crop, urging her into a gallop. The wind blew sharp against her face, and the ground slid below her in a blur of motion. The faster Nugget ran, the more Katherine loved it. All her troubles flew away, left behind by the speed of her magnificent horse.

By the time Katherine slowed Nugget to a walk and started back, dark shadows lurked in the leafless oak woods on each side of the trail. Katherine's mind started up again, nagged by a dozen little worries. She thought of all those ladies who flounced about Victoria in their fashionable dresses with their long, hooped skirts so wide they sometimes had difficulty squeezing through doorways. They looked down on her, those British wives and daughters, thinking her a poor farm girl from the wild colony of British Columbia.

Emma Curtis was one of them. Emma thought herself of a better class; Katherine saw it in the way Emma always kept her distance and refused to look directly at her. Perhaps more telling was her manner of speaking. The way Emma pronounced each word with such dreadful slowness made Katherine cringe, as if the girl thought Katherine would not understand if she spoke too quickly.

Although she didn't wear hooped skirts, Emma's clothes were of excellent quality, if slightly out of date. And she wore that beautiful ring. Katherine had scarcely been able to drag her eyes away when Emma lifted her hand to stroke Nugget. She had never before seen such a ring on a girl of Emma's age.

Obviously she came from an upper-class family, but even so there was something mysterious about Emma, as if the girl kept a dark secret hidden so deep within her no one would ever find it. Some great sadness perhaps, or a fear she could never admit to having. And those eyes. As much as Katherine wanted to dismiss Emma as a snob, her eyes – so big and dark they should have been beautiful – instead held a haunted look in them.

What was Mr. Bentley's role in all of this? Why should he buy a horse for Emma? The two had a similar look about them, both being tall and thin with dark hair and eyes. Could they be related in some way? Perhaps he was an uncle on Emma's mother's side, since he had a different last name. Emma had never once mentioned her parents, and Katherine had an idea she didn't live with them. Yes, there was certainly a mystery surrounding Emma Curtis. Katherine considered asking next time she saw Emma but decided against it. That girl was too standoffish to welcome questions from a near stranger.

Partway up the gentle slope leading to the barn, Katherine glimpsed a dark figure lurking near the open door, almost hidden in shadow. Nugget whinnied, and Katherine reined her in, unsure what to do.

"Is that you, Miss Harris?" Mr. Bentley's voice floated out of the darkness.

Not certain whether to be relieved or apprehensive, she urged Nugget forward.

Mr. Bentley followed her to the stall, where she went about grooming her horse, a process that normally relaxed her and Nugget both. Today was different. Today Nugget snorted uneasily and her skin flinched where Katherine touched it with the currycomb. Katherine knew it was her own tension that passed itself through to the horse. It was Mr. Bentley's fault. Must he stand behind them watching her every move? What did want from her?

"Miss Harris," he said at last, "I wonder if you can tell me if Emma came by today?"

Oh, so it was information he was after. Katherine considered her answer. She did not want to lie to this man, and yet she did not fancy acting as his spy either. "She did."

"Did she take an interest in the horse?"

"Yes." With long, quick strokes, Katherine continued brushing Nugget's coat.

He waited. When Katherine said no more, he asked, "All right then, what did she do?"

She stopped brushing. "Emma fed Nugget an apple."

"Aha! Then it is working! I knew my idea was a good one and Emma's curiosity would get the better of her."

Katherine glanced over her shoulder. Mr. Bentley rose up on his toes and back down, a pleased smile splitting his beard. She turned back to Nugget, too angry to speak. Too angry to remind him that the idea was Edward's and not his at all.

"And is she ready to try riding?"

"No. Not yet. You can't rush her into something she isn't ready for."

She became aware of Mr. Bentley's silence. She looked

over her shoulder, let her gaze travel up and over his crossed arms all the way up to his face. What she saw was a heavy beard and two thick eyebrows pulled low over dark and threatening eyes.

"Miss Harris, I'll have you know that I am not trying to force Emma into anything." His voice was tight and angry. "But the fact is, she must be a good rider by next spring when we will be travelling into British Columbia to start our farm."

Oh. Starting a farm together? Emma Curtis and Joseph Bentley? Why would Emma want to leave her comfortable life in Victoria? None of this made any sense at all.

When Katherine didn't reply but only stood there gaping up at him, Mr. Bentley uncrossed his arms, glared over his beard, then turned and walked briskly from the barn.

***

Friday morning Katherine sat in her school room, gazing out the window. Rain streamed down through low grey cloud, making ghosts of the graceful cedar trees not twenty feet away. It thundered against the roof, a sad, depressing sound.

"Miss Harris!"

Her head jerked back from the window.

Mr. Brett studied her from behind his desk. "Pray tell me, Miss Harris, is the work so boring that you must look for inspiration outside the window?"

All the students paused, every eye turned to Katherine. Her cheeks flushed warm. "No, sir. But you see, I..."

"If you would stop staring out the window and start

paying attention to your lessons, you might get some-where," Mr. Brett said, and his hard eyes glittered.

"But I have finished all the work you gave me, sir."

"Impossible!"

Katherine didn't answer. A student must never argue with a teacher. Mr. Brett was a man who did everything quickly. He strutted about the room and often talked so fast it was difficult to understand him. And he could lose his temper in the blink of an eye. He stormed over to her now. "Let me see what you have done!"

Katherine handed him her work. He trotted back to his desk, sat down and checked it over, making large quick marks on the paper. "Miss Harris," he said, "come to my desk immediately."

Fingers interlaced on the desk in front of him, he watched Katherine make her way to the front of the room. She couldn't imagine what she had done wrong, the work was so simple. Every eye in the classroom fol-lowed her, most of them happy to see her in trouble. One step, another, and another after that, the aisle seemed endlessly long.

Mr. Brett handed back her work and Katherine saw in a glance that she had made no mistakes. She looked up in surprise. Why was she in trouble?

"Well done," he said, folding his chubby arms on his desk. He glanced up sharply at her classmates. "You could all learn a lesson from Miss Harris here. Now, stop your staring and get back to work."

The teacher was a small man with a round red face, wide, sloppy mouth, and thin brown hair combed straight back from his forehead. "I can see you are far ad-vanced over all the other students in this classroom. May

DAYLE CAMPBELL GAETZ

I ask where you were educated?"

"Yes," Katherine said. "I grew up in England, where my father saw to it that we were well schooled. He believes education is necessary to better oneself in life." *Even if only to entrap a higher class of husband.*

"Quite right," Mr. Brett agreed. He looked at the class again. "I hope you all heard what Miss Harris here has to say."

Katherine cringed. If she had difficulty fitting in until now, Mr. Brett's praise could only make matters worse.

"Please return to your seat, Miss Harris, while I work out a way for you to use your time with us profitably."

Katherine returned to her seat. The distance seemed even further now, with the older students glaring at her every step of the way. She sat down and studied the scratched surface of her desk.

"You think you're so smart!" The whisper came from behind.

Katherine glanced over her shoulder. Even with her thin eyebrows pulled close together over her wide blue eyes and her mouth turned down in a hard line, Margaret Steeves still looked pretty. Fifteen-year-old Margaret had light blonde hair and soft pink and white skin. When Katherine had first seen Margaret, she was reminded of Susan and hoped they might become friends. But this girl was nothing like Susan. Nothing at all. Margaret was cruel and vain, while Susan had been the kindest person in the entire world.

In spite of Margaret's harsh nature, the other pupils looked up to her. Whatever Margaret liked, they liked. Whatever Margaret did not like, they did not like. And Margaret Steeves did not like Katherine.

"It's not that I am smart," Katherine tried to explain. "It's only that I've done all of this work before. We had a tutor in England, that's why it's easy for me." A sudden idea occurred to her. "I'll help you if you like," she offered.

Margaret rolled her eyes. "I'd rather die," she said, loud enough for everyone to hear. "What makes you think I need help anyway?"

"I only thought," Katherine stumbled over her words, "if you believe I'm so smart you must be having difficulty."

"Is there a problem here, Miss Steeves?"

Katherine whirled around. Mr. Brett loomed over the two of them.

"This wretched little farm girl offered to help me with my schoolwork. Me!" Margaret said, as though the very idea were preposterous.

The teacher sighed. "While I'm certain you could learn a lot from Miss Harris," he said, "I don't think it fair to ask such a formidable task of her."

He turned to Katherine. "I'm hoping Miss Harris will agree to helping out with the younger pupils?"

"Of course, sir, I'd love to." She'd be happy to get away from Margaret, if only for a short time.

For the first time since Katherine had joined his classroom, Mr. Brett smiled. "Thank you, I appreciate it. In the meantime, I shall look into providing you with more challenging work."

"I would like that." She stood up and crossed a silent classroom with every eye trained on her. She felt Margaret Steeves' eyes burning into her back.

DAYLE CAMPBELL GAETZ

Saturday afternoon, Katherine stood at the window of the small library in the Morris house, watching rain pound against the glass, blurring and distorting the outside world. She heard a footstep and turned to see Mrs. Morris flounce down the stairs. At the bottom she stopped to check her reflection in the mirror. She adjusted her hat and pulled on her gloves, admiring herself all the while.

Katherine pretended to be engrossed by Mr. Morris' books that still lined the shelves. Accounting books for the most part, which might interest Mother, but Katherine had yet to find one book she wanted to read. She listened for the sound of the door closing behind Mrs. Morris. What was keeping her?

"Still moping around the house I see," Mrs. Morris said in her high-pitched, nasal voice. "Honestly Katherine, I simply do not understand you. When I was your age it was one party after another, picnics, tennis. We had such a wonderful time!"

"This is not a very good day for a picnic," Katherine pointed out, "and I haven't been invited to any parties."

"Now that's not true, Katherine. You know Mrs. Steeves specifically invited you in person just yesterday when she was here for tea. She has a daughter about your age and was kind enough to include you in a gathering in her home. But you, rather rudely I might say, refused."

"Only because I know Margaret and she doesn't like me. She would not be pleased to see me in her home." Katherine didn't add that Margaret would see to it that the occasion was as wretched as possible for her.

Mrs. Morris pursed her mouth. She was only a few

years older than Katherine's mother, but while Mrs. Harris was still slender and young looking, Mrs. Morris's waist and hips were thick from all the sweets she ate, and she had the beginnings of a double chin. "And what makes you say such a thing? Margaret is a lovely, gracious girl, and pretty too. I expect she has plenty of friends and admirers even if her parents don't have money enough to send her to a suitable school. Not with all those boys of theirs who need a proper education."

Margaret has lots of friends who do her bidding, Katherine thought but could not say. She must not upset Mrs. Morris, who would go running to Mrs. Steeves and tell her everything. Mrs. Steeves would surely tell Margaret, who would find new ways to make Katherine's school life miserable. "I expect you're right," she agreed.

Mrs. Morris took her umbrella from the stand near the door. With one hand on the door handle, she glanced back at Katherine. "Yes, well, I shall be off then."

Relieved that Mrs. Morris didn't press the matter, Katherine spent a few more minutes searching the shelves, then hurried upstairs to change her clothes. She would go to Beckley Farm and visit Nugget in spite of the rain.

Sunday morning, Katherine sat in church beside Mrs. Morris. Being early, she used the time to watch people file in. James Douglas, Governor of Vancouver Island and British Columbia, strode down the aisle in his dark suit and high starched collar. His grey hair curled down his neck but was in short supply over his forehead. Thick white sideburns grew almost to his chin. As if he sensed

Katherine watching, he turned her way, his face stern, a sad look to his round dark eyes. Beside him walked his wife Amelia, kind-faced and matronly, her black hair mostly hidden by her bonnet. Their two youngest children, James and Martha, followed close behind. And behind them someone else. A tall young woman who looked like – yes, indeed, it was – Emma Curtis! The Douglas family settled in their pew at the front of the church, leaving Katherine to speculate.

It seemed she was right. Emma did not live with her parents at all but with the Douglas family. Since Emma wasn't one of their daughters, who were all married now except little Martha, Katherine decided she must be a niece. As often happened, Emma likely had been sent from a remote Hudson's Bay fort to stay with relatives while she completed her schooling at an expensive school for girls.

Still, that didn't explain why Emma was more free to do as she pleased than other young women who had two parents watching their every move. Katherine studied the back of the governor's head. From what she knew of him, he was an exacting man who expected all around him to behave with the strictest of etiquette. Which meant any relative living in his care would be held to the highest possible standards.

Katherine's thoughts were interrupted by the arrival of the Steeves family. They settled directly behind her and Mrs. Morris.

"The nerve of that girl!" Mrs. Steeves said in a whisper meant to be overheard. "Imagine turning down an invitation to *our* home!"

"Katherine Harris has disliked me from the day she arrived, Mama. I suspect she is jealous of our social position."

"I expect you're right, dear. Of course, I only invited her out of the goodness of my heart. I felt sorry for the poor, dreary child."

The service began, and Katherine blocked the two of them from her mind. During the interminable sermon, she fixed her eyes on a church window, hoping for some sign the endless rain had stopped. Finally, as the last hymn began, a glimmer of sunlight sparkled through the glass. Katherine could hardly wait to get out there.

It was mid afternoon before she managed to get away, having told Mrs. Morris that she was going for a walk in the sunshine. Not that Mrs. Morris cared where she went, the only reason the widow allowed Katherine to stay with her at all was to collect the room and board Katherine's parents paid her.

Katherine had the sidesaddle on Nugget and was bent over to cinch it up when she heard footsteps approaching. She recognized them immediately. The little shuffle, as if her leg hurt, gave Emma away and made Katherine smile to herself. Edward was right: Simply let her alone, allow her to choose her own time, and Emma would soon show an interest in the horse. "Did you bring an apple?"

"No, I...uh, not today."

Katherine straightened up and reached for the bridle. Should she ask if Emma wanted to try riding today? Would that be pushing her? This girl was far too sensitive for her own good. Katherine had figured that out by now, and so she hesitated to ask any unnecessary questions. Right now Emma was gazing at Nugget with such a faraway look in her eyes Katherine wondered if she saw the horse at all. Emma looked unhappy, and Katherine thought she knew why. "Mr. Bentley tells me you're going off to start a farm next spring," she ventured.

Emma blinked. She turned to Katherine with a mixture of surprise and confusion on her face. "I'm considering it," she said in her slow and guarded way. She turned toward the door, dismissing Katherine.

All right then, Katherine thought, *if that's the way she wants to be, then fine.* There was no point in trying to get to know this Emma Curtis, who made it quite plain she had no interest in talking to her. From now on she would simply take care of Nugget and stay clear of this unfriendly girl.

"Has Tall Joe been by here lately?" Emma asked, still eyeing the door.

"Tall Joe?"

"I mean Mr. Bentley. I call him Tall Joe because that's the name he got up in the Cariboo, where he mined for gold."

"Oh, I see. The name suits him, don't you think?"

Emma turned back to Katherine but didn't reply.

Katherine almost changed her mind then. She almost asked Emma why she would want to leave Victoria and go off to start a farm with this Mr. Bentley, who seemed so gruff. But Nugget chose that moment to paw the ground and snort her impatience.

Emma jumped back.

"Don't worry, Emma, Nugget is only anxious to get going. She needs a good run."

Emma watched Katherine lead the horse from the stall. On her walk to the farm today, Emma had considered trying to sit on the horse, in the yard, with no one watching and Katherine holding the reins. But now she changed her mind. She would be daft to climb on such a wild beast, snorting and pawing the ground as it was, and under the control of a girl who seemed to think that great beast should belong to her. Well, but Tall Joe bought the horse and gave it to Emma, whether either girl liked it or not.

At the door, Katherine stopped and looked back. "I have an idea," she said. "Why don't I take Nugget for a run on the track at Beacon Hill and come back? Once she has burned up some of her energy, she'll be much calmer, and you can try riding her."

Emma walked toward the door, giving herself time to think. This Katherine might be confused, but she did know about horses, and that's for certain-sure. "I might try it today," she said, "but I shall follow you to the track. I want to watch the horse gallop and see how you ride without bouncing off on your head."

"All right then." Katherine led Nugget to the block and climbed into the saddle. She bent her right leg around the pommel.

Emma stared at that saddle, at Katherine's right knee twisted around that curved pommel. She felt ill. Her own poor knee ached at the thought of bending so sharply.

Katherine studied her face. "I have a perfectly marvelous idea," she said. "I don't expect anyone will be about and I have yet to see a soul on the track at this time of day. So I'm going to take off this sidesaddle and ride the way I find most comfortable."

She dismounted, led Nugget back inside, tied her reins to a post, and set about switching saddles. "You must promise not to tell," Katherine said, when she had the new saddle in place.

"I promise," Emma whispered.

Back at the block, Katherine hitched up her long skirt and swung her leg smoothly over the horse's back to ride astride. Her full skirt bunched over the horse's withers and hung down to the tops of her boots. She tapped Nugget with her heels. "I'll see you soon, then."

Emma's stomach twisted in alarm. "Wait!" she cried, raising her hand, desperate to change her mind.

But Katherine trotted off, looking straight ahead, sitting gracefully in the saddle, with its high back and saddle horn at the front. Emma's hand fell to her side.

She followed in the direction Katherine had gone, wanting with every step to turn around and walk as fast as she could in the other direction. But she would rather die than have that Katherine girl think she was scared. So she continued on, making every effort to disguise her uneven gait. One wrong step and she'd find herself lying in the slippery muck they called a road, and that's for certain-sure.

10

Katherine slowed Nugget and approached the track cautiously, peering in every direction. "Just as I hoped, girl," she said. "There's not a soul here, no one to raise a fuss over my choice of a man's saddle – which is none of their concern anyway, if you ask me." She tapped her horse lightly with her heels.

Nugget needed no further encouragement. She stretched her neck, lengthened her stride, and galloped around the track, fairly vibrating with joy. That joy passed itself on to Katherine, who tossed off all her worries and thought of nothing except the sun on her face, the wind in her hair, and her wonderful, magnificent horse.

When Nugget began to tire, Katherine pulled gently on the reins and trotted toward the trail where Emma should be waiting. But even now the girl was nowhere in sight. It seemed she was not going to show up after all. No one could take so long to walk such a short distance.

"I simply don't understand that girl," Katherine told Nugget, "but at least now we have time to explore that path I noticed. I wonder where it goes?"

She walked Nugget along the edge of the trees until she spotted a path that she had glimpsed earlier, as Nugget galloped by. Almost hidden beneath a stand of young oaks and dense undergrowth, the narrow path wound its way into the woods.

"Easy now, Nugget," she whispered, ducking to clear low-hanging branches. Like the prow of a steamer, Nugget's shoulders pushed aside a sea of undergrowth, swishing and crackling around her. As Katherine had hoped, the path continued in the general direction of Beckley Farm. "This looks perfect," she whispered. "I expect it will provide exactly what we need."

Katherine followed the path for a few minutes longer, until a sudden thought struck her. At the same moment, Nugget stopped walking. Had Katherine pulled back on the reins? She didn't think so. "Did you think of it too?" she asked. "Or are you so tuned in to my thoughts you stop without being told?"

Turning around wasn't easy on this narrow path. Dense undergrowth closed in on every side, but after a few minutes of jockeying back and forth they were headed back toward the park.

"How stupid of me," Katherine said. "Of course Emma will take longer than most people. As much as she tries to hide it, there is something quite wrong with Emma's right leg, and did you see the way she stared up at the sidesaddle with her eyes wide like a frightened deer? I know it hurts her, but she's so proud I'm afraid she'll only get angry if I dare ask what's wrong."

They arrived back at the track in time to see Emma emerge from the trees, picking her way over the uneven ground. Katherine trotted Nugget toward her. "You're just at the right time," she called. "Nugget had a good run and she's not so bursting with energy now."

Emma looked up uncertainly, as if she would change

her mind again.

"But if you're too frightened..."

"I am not frightened of anything," Emma informed her.

"All right then." Katherine led Nugget to a large, flat rock and dismounted.

"I'll hold her steady while you climb on. Remember, you always mount a horse from her left side. That's what they're trained to expect."

Emma nodded and climbed onto the rock.

"Good, now grab hold of the saddle horn and the back of her saddle...put the toe of your left boot in the stirrup... You're doing well! Now, pull yourself up and ease your right leg over the horse. And you're there!"

Sitting high up in the saddle, Emma looked down at Katherine, her face flushed warm with pride. "That was not so bad as I thought it would be!"

"I think you're a natural-born horsewoman," Katherine told her. "Now let me lead you around a few times, and then you can take the reins yourself."

Emma's lips twitched.

"Don't worry, Nugget is very well trained. She'll do exactly as you tell her."

Liberty, Emma almost corrected but changed her mind. With her sitting up so high and wobbly in the saddle and Katherine down there holding the reins, this did not seem a good time to make the girl angry.

Half an hour later, Emma was seated quite comfortably on Liberty and was walking the horse around the grassy field on her own. By laying the reins one way or another across Liberty's neck, she could make the horse turn left or right. A gentle tug and the horse stopped. If she had known it was this easy, she would have tried sooner.

As if reading her mind, Katherine called out, "There's more to riding a horse than simply walking her! Are you ready to try a trot?"

And why not? What was a trot if it wasn't just a faster way of walking? "Of course," she called back. "What shall I do?"

Katherine ran to catch up. Jogging alongside the horse she said, "Remember, a trot is a very rough ride. It takes a lot of getting used to, so you won't want to do it for long. When you're ready, tap Nugget's sides very gently with your heels – not too hard unless you want her to canter – and don't forget, when you want her to slow down again, simply pull on the reins as you did to make her stop." She paused. "All right?"

Emma nodded. "It sounds rather simple to me." She tapped Liberty's sides. The next thing Emma knew she was bouncing up and down on the horse's back until she was sure every tooth in her head would rattle clean out of her jaws and every bone in her body would split apart. The horse went down, Emma bounced up. The horse bounced back up, Emma came down with a painful jolt. Up she went again. This may have been a mistake. Ow! This was a mistake. Ow! What now? Tap Liberty's sides? Ow! No. She couldn't think. Ow! Her brain rattled in her skull. Ow! Her hip hurt so badly. Ow! She was going to bounce clean off the saddle. Ow again!

"Whoa there, Nugget. Whoa, girl!" At the sound of Katherine's voice, the horse slowed and came to a stop.

Nugget lowered her head and snorted her disapproval of the rider on her back.

Emma's entire body trembled. If trotting was so difficult, what chance did she have at a gallop, or even a canter?

Katherine caught up, breathless. She held Nugget's reins and stroked her muzzle. "Good Nugget," she said. "Good horse." Then she looked up at Emma. "I'm sorry," she said. "I should never have suggested trotting so soon. Are you all right?"

Emma lifted her chin. "I am fine."

"Good then." Katherine grinned. "Do you want to try again?"

Emma clutched the saddlehorn. Tried to stop her hands from shaking.

"I did warn you it would be a rough ride." Katherine's eyes twinkled. She looked up at Emma, half-laughing.

Emma felt a quick stab of anger. There was nothing funny about what just happened. She could have been killed! Shaken to her death on the back of a bouncing horse. Her bones split into a thousand pieces. Then, unaccountably, she felt a smile steal over her own cheeks. "Well, and you were right!"

Katherine's face crinkled and her eyes became little crescent moons. She laughed all the way from her stomach. Emma found herself joining in and quickly discovered that laughing while sitting shakily in a saddle with a sore and tender backside did not mix well. And that made her laugh all the harder. "Oh," she said. "Oh! Ow!"

Emma could not fathom what happened next. One second, Katherine was laughing up at her, the next she gasped aloud and slapped a hand over her mouth. Her face contorted as if in pain. She slipped a hand into the pocket of her dress and pulled out a small cloth bag.

"Are you ill?" Emma asked.

Katherine swiped at tears that spilled from her eyes. Her fingers curled tight around the bag. "I'm fine."

Emma's laughter stuck in her throat. *It must be the horse,* she thought. *The girl is that upset to see me seated on her horse. And it's not my fault, it's Tall Joe who bought the horse and Mayor Harris who sold it.* She tried to think what to say, but nothing seemed right and she couldn't apologize for something neither of them could change. "Perhaps I'll stick to walking the horse for today," she said.

Katherine nodded, staring at the ground. "That seems a good plan."

"You'll want to dismount before we reach the farm," Katherine advised, leading Nugget home with Emma riding. "You will need to stretch your legs so you don't stumble."

"Why should I stumble?" Emma snapped.

"Everyone is sore the first time they ride," Katherine explained, wondering why Emma sounded so cross. "Your legs will feel weak and shaky when you first dismount and I don't expect you'll want to fall on your face in the event Tall Joe or Edward are watching."

To make Emma feel better, Katherine decided to tell her about that first day in Hope. She stopped and turned around. Emma scowled down as if she couldn't stand the sight of her. But Katherine was getting used to Emma's quick changes in mood, so she went ahead anyway. "Wait until you hear what happened to me. It was the first time

I had ridden sidesaddle since we left England and the first time I had worn a skirt for some time. I rode into Hope with my brother and..."

Katherine related how she had tumbled from the saddle in front of those three strangers and her bonnet fell off and George stuffed it back on her head all crooked and with her short hair sticking out from under it. She lifted her hat then, the hat she always wore, to show Emma how short her hair still was.

Emma's grumpy look melted, the corners of her mouth twitched, and her eyes crinkled. Laughing, Katherine struggled to finish telling her story. But as soon as she was done, memories of Susan came flooding back, memories of the carefree laughter they used to share. What was wrong with her today? Had she forgotten her sister so easily?

Emma could not recall ever laughing so hard. There had been little to laugh about in her life. It felt good, she decided. It filled her with a warmth that remained long after the laughter ended. She was intrigued by Katherine's story and wanted to ask what the girl was doing up in Hope, who had cut her hair so short, and how could she not have been wearing a skirt? More than anything she wanted to know how Katherine had been allowed to use a man's saddle.

But Katherine had stopped laughing so abruptly Emma decided to keep quiet. Something was bothering that girl. Emma didn't know what, but she had never been one to pry and wasn't about to start now. "I shall take your advice then," Emma said, "and get down from the horse right here."

Katherine held Nugget still. She explained how to dismount and Emma managed to lower herself to the ground without falling. But the moment she stepped away from the horse, she knew Katherine was right. Her legs wouldn't straighten out properly. They felt numb and shaky, as if they would give out beneath her if she tried to take a step.

An unexpected laugh burst out of her. Seemed like this laughing business was an odd sort of thing; once you got started, you did it more and more. "Can you just see the look on Tall Joe's face if I fell in the mud at his feet?" Emma pulled herself up tall, threw her head back, rubbed a hand over an imaginary beard, and glared down at Katherine, eyebrows raised.

"But – you look exactly like him!"

"I look like my mother," Emma snapped. "Not Tall Joe!"

"I only meant you imitated his expression so well."

"Mrs. Douglas says I have his eyes, but I don't want them."

Katherine stared at her. "Emma, why should you have his eyes in the first place? Is he a relation?"

"Turns out the man is my father." *Ahh.* And now she had done it.

"Oh!" Katherine stammered. "I thought..."

Emma felt trapped on this narrow path with no way out but past Katherine. And those eyes gaping like her tongue had gotten stuck in her throat. But not for long enough.

"Then how is it your last name's Curtis and not Bentley? Where is your mother? Why do you live with the Douglas family and not your own father?"

The girl asked too many questions, and that's for certain-sure. Emma wasn't about to tell her how Tall Joe ran off with a promise to return and marry her mother when he was rich enough and neither one knew there was a baby on the way. This Katherine would look down on her if she learned of the shame her mother had endured at the hands of polite society. Jenny Curtis, a girl not yet eighteen, was kicked out of her home by her own father, a pastor, who never did speak to her again. Her mother had made her way to Manchester and the workhouse but later ran away so they couldn't take Emma from her. She had raised Emma on her own, with never enough to eat until she died on the floor of a nethersken and never once heard from Tall Joe in all that time. "I grew up believing my father was dead," Emma said at last. "It was only by chance I found him living here after I arrived."

"Oh!" Katherine bit her lip, opened her mouth, and slapped it shut again. She frowned up at Emma. "So then, if he's your father, and he wants to take care of you now... how old are you, Emma?"

"Almost fourteen."

Katherine's eyebrows rose. "I guess your father is trying to make up for his past mistakes?"

Emma shrugged. "Can we go now? I'm cold."

"But..." Katherine stared at Emma.

Emma felt her face twist up with pain, but this Katherine kept staring, bursting with too many questions. Well, and Emma knew how to stop her. She opened her mouth to make an angry retort.

Before she could speak, Katherine's face softened. "All right then," she said, and led Nugget away.

Emma limped along behind.

"No one's in sight," Katherine whispered as they neared the barn. "I'll whip this saddle off Nugget and no one will ever know the difference."

"I shall be on my way then," Emma said stiffly. "Thank you for the riding lesson, Katherine."

"Will you be back tomorrow?"

"No, I am unable to return again until Wednesday."

The sky was black, the air gathering cold when Emma reached the back door. Inside, she was greeted by a welcome warmth and the enticing aroma of duck roasting in the oven. Mrs. Douglas, with little Martha beside her, turned from the woodstove, her broad face flushed with the heat, black hair pulled back in a bun. "You must be cold, Emma. There's tea made."

Mrs. Douglas placed cups and saucers and a plate of little cakes on the table.

"How is your horse today?" she asked, lowering herself to a chair across from Emma.

Martha joined them, her eyes on the cakes.

"But how could you know where I've been?"

"You smell like a horse," Martha said, wrinkling her nose.

"Oh."

They sat in comfortable silence, broken only by the creak of Martha's chair as her short legs swung back and forth beneath the table. Emma reached for a second cake. Even after all this time, she never could eat something so delicious without a sense of wonder, without marveling at how lucky she was to have so much food and never a hungry day.

After Martha excused herself and ran off, Emma could wait no longer. "I did it!" she said. "I rode..." She was about to say *Liberty,* but something held her back, some sense that Mrs. Douglas would not approve of her changing the horse's name. "...I rode the horse, at a walk at least."

Once started, Emma found herself telling Mrs. Douglas all about the horse, and Katherine's help, and how truly horrid it felt when the horse began to trot.

Mrs. Douglas nodded. "I worried about your leg. It must hurt, bending in that cramped position on the sidesaddle."

Emma hesitated. She reached for a third cake but no longer felt like eating. She put the cake on her plate and leaned across the table. "I didn't use a sidesaddle."

Mrs. Douglas frowned. She sipped her tea. "Was that Katherine's idea?"

Emma pushed the uneaten cake around her plate. If she answered 'Yes,' would Katherine be in trouble?

"Because, if it was, she must be a very understanding young lady."

"I suppose."

"And a good friend."

Friend? Emma Curtis did not need a friend. And never one so proper as that Miss Katherine Harris.

Mrs. Douglas leaned in close. "You must be careful though. Governor Douglas would be shocked if he knew about the saddle. And as for your father..."

"Horrified!" Emma pursed her lips, tossed back her head, rubbed an imaginary beard, and glared down her nose.

They both laughed. Mrs. Douglas said nothing about Emma's looking like Tall Joe when she made that face.

Emma stood to clear the dishes away. She was washing up when Mrs. Douglas said, "You must go every afternoon to practice riding, Emma. You need to be ready when your father and Ned Turner make up their minds to go in search of land."

Emma clutched a soapy saucer in both hands. Her first thought was to object. She wanted to say that, really, she should be working at that time of day, and didn't Mrs. Douglas need her? She placed the saucer to drain and glanced over her shoulder. The look on her employer's face revealed how happy Mrs. Douglas was to give her this gift. A gift of time.

"And don't worry about your work," Mrs. Douglas added. "It's time Martha began helping out after school. Her older sisters knew how to cook and clean at Martha's age.

"Thank you," Emma said. "I'll do my best to learn and hope it doesn't hurt too bad." She hobbled across the room to pick up the cakes, exaggerating her limp, rubbing her backside as she went.

Mrs. Douglas glanced at her in quick surprise. They both laughed again.

Emma had never laughed so much in one day in her entire life before. She was amazed how good it made her feel.

11

True to his word, Mr. Brett prepared lessons that would challenge Katherine. She read novels and discussed them with the teacher while the other pupils worked. She studied history texts but especially enjoyed reading maps and learning about faraway places in her geography lessons. She marveled that so many countries around the world were a part of the British Empire, as were these two colonies on the western edge of North America.

Katherine spent part of every school day teaching the younger pupils. She learned how to explain things in a way that made it easy for the children to understand. Seeing a child's face light up when he suddenly realized he could read the words in front of him gave her a warm sense of satisfaction. And because she was accomplishing so much, Katherine no longer cared what Margaret Steeves and the other pupils thought of her. She had come to Victoria to improve her education, and that was what she intended to do. Maybe, if she worked hard enough this year, she could gain enough education to open that little school she and Susan had dreamed of, for children too young to be away from their parents.

Thursday afternoon, as she practiced printing with a group of eight-year-olds, Katherine could not resist glancing out the window every few minutes. And each time she was delighted to see the sun still shining, the air still and clear and inviting. She could hardly wait for school to be over. Today she would have Nugget all to herself.

Half an hour after school ended, Katherine had the sidesaddle on Nugget. She was leading the horse outside when Emma appeared. Katherine couldn't hide her disappointment. "What are you doing here?" she snapped.

Emma sucked in her breath. She lifted her chin and narrowed her eyes. "Mrs. Douglas says I should come every day to practice riding so I shall be ready to travel by spring."

Katherine grimaced. Every day? She had so looked forward to this time alone with Nugget. And by next spring the horse would be gone. "I've already saddled her."

"I see that."

"She needs a good run."

"Yes."

Katherine watched Emma, willing her to leave. Emma shuffled her feet on the dirt floor. Her eyes wandered from Katherine to the horse and back again as if she weren't quite sure what to do.

Finally Katherine's sense of fairness won over. "Wait," she said. "I have an idea." She went to the tack room and came back carrying a bridle and the sidesaddle they had used the day before. She put the saddle down and took the bridle into a stall.

A few minutes later she led the short, light grey horse out. The mare's head hung low as if her neck were tired of holding it up. She plodded along on short, bony legs that looked like they had not supported a rider in many years.

"This is Princess," Katherine announced. "She's nineteen

years old and much smaller than Nugget, but Edward told me she's stronger than she looks and has the smoothest ride of any horse on all of Vancouver Island. She has the best temperament too, so she's perfect for a beginning rider and especially for learning how to trot without too much pain."

"Good!" Emma said with so much enthusiasm that Katherine chuckled.

"You might be a wee bit sore from yesterday?"

Emma nodded. "More than a wee bit, if you want to know."

"Fine. We'll take it easy today." Katherine smiled, relieved she had found a way to include Emma without giving up Nugget so soon.

With Katherine leading both horses and Emma following behind, they walked toward a narrow, overgrown path leading into a thick cedar forest. "No one is likely to see us on this path," Katherine said, stopping near a large stump. "I'm hoping it meets up with the path I noticed yesterday before you arrived."

She helped Emma onto Princess and handed her the reins. "How does that feel?" she asked.

"Not so bad." Emma pulled on the reins in an attempt to raise the horse's head. Princess took no notice. "This horse won't likely go galloping off with me crying out for her to stop."

"No," Katherine agreed, "but you may soon be crying for her to get moving."

For the next fifteen minutes, the two horses wound through a tangle of undergrowth. Katherine glanced back often to see Emma holding the reins in one hand, the other clutching the saddlehorn. The grey horse moped along, head scarcely above the thick bushes.

The path emerged on a deserted meadow leading to a hillside dotted with Garry oaks. "We did it," Katherine said. "We found a secret path to the track below Beacon Hill."

Nugget pranced into the meadow, tossing her head and tugging on the reins. Katherine turned to Emma. "Nugget needs her exercise. Will you be all right on your own until we get back?"

Emma nodded. "I shall be fine."

She would be, Emma told herself. She would be fine. Quite all right. Even so, her stomach did somersaults just thinking of being alone with the horse in this wide open space.

"Good then, we'll be off." Katherine flicked the reins and sped away.

Emma watched horse and rider soar along the track so fast Liberty's black tail flew straight out behind. She envied the way Katherine sat so comfortably in the saddle while the horse's dark legs blurred and her heels kicked up little clods of grass and damp earth. Princess watched too, and her head sank lower, as if the very sight exhausted her.

Emma thought of her mother, old and tired before her time. Her eyes slid down to the ring, admiring the way it glowed. If Mam could see her now, would she be proud? Tall Joe said her mother had been a good rider. Emma tapped the horse's sides, and Princess began a slow plod around the field. "I'm tryin', Mam," she whispered. Then, remembering her promise to speak properly, added,

"Mama, I'm doing my best to make you proud of me."

Twice around the track and Emma was beginning to get bored. Maybe she should try a trot. Now, with no one to see her fail, was the perfect time. Emma tapped Princess with her heels and flicked the reins, bracing herself for what was to come.

Princess might have increased her pace, but it was difficult to say for certain. Emma tried again. She tapped a little harder with the heels of her boots and jerked the reins with more force. Princess stopped altogether. She twisted her neck to look up at Emma.

"An' it's high time you did as I say unless you fancy endin' up in the glue factory," Emma warned.

As if she understood, Princess raised her head and started to walk, picking up speed until Emma found herself bouncing along on the horse's back. Princess might be trotting, but Emma soon realized she was still in control – sort of. She bounced up, landed. Stayed with the horse for a few steps. Bounced up again. It was true. Princess was smoother than Liberty. Easier to keep from colliding with. Easier to control. Oh, ow! But only if Emma concentrated. Better. Good. Stay with the horse. Not so bad. Not so bad. Oh, no! Ow! What happened?

Emma's brain rattled. Enough of this. Do something. Now. She pulled on the reins. Princess stopped and dropped her head, tossing Emma forward in the saddle.

She clutched the saddlehorn in both hands and sat completely still. Princess didn't move either. Horse and rider both breathed hard, relieved to no longer be trotting. Emma heard hoofbeats and looked up to see Katherine heading her way.

"An' I hope she never did see that performance," she

whispered. "Let's get moving, old girl." She tapped Princess with her heels, and the horse plodded on. Better bored than battered, Emma thought. Better bored than battered.

They returned to Beckley Farm by the same secret path, swishing through undergrowth too dark to see. A glow of lantern light spilled from the barn door.

"Could you hold Princess while I get Nugget settled?" Katherine asked, leading Nugget to her stall.

Emma nodded. Her heart might beat too fast and her breath stick in her throat with the horse looming so close behind her, but she would not let Katherine see. She forced herself to stand still, tried to look unconcerned, and wished Katherine would hurry up.

A warm hand touched hers where she held the reins. Emma whirled around. "Edward!"

"I knew you'd done it," he whispered. "I knew you had gone off and not used the sidesaddle!"

"But..."

"Good idea. It must be easier for you, uh, I mean for anyone to learn that way."

"Yes."

"But Mr. Bentley now, I don't suppose he'll like it so much."

"No, he, uh..."

"He has his set ideas on how young ladies should behave."

"Yes," Emma agreed.

"Let me take care of Princess for you," he said, and took the reins from her hand.

Emma followed. "I'll be needing to get back now," she told him.

"What's your hurry? You've got to stay a while at least. We need to make some plans."

"What sort of plans?"

Edward turned his attention to the horse. "You might have noticed Mr. Bentley hasn't been stopping by here in the last few days?"

"I have, and...?"

"I might have, uh, suggested that if he left you alone for a while, you might try riding on your own."

"Well, and looks like it worked," Emma snapped. And who did he think he was, scheming behind her back, she'd like to know? Emma tried to scowl at him but surprised herself by laughing out loud. What was wrong with her these days, laughing when she meant to be cross?

Edward glanced up, eyebrows raised. His face broke into a wide smile. "We need to keep Mr. Bentley from finding out about, um...the saddle and all."

Her throat tightened. Tall Joe wanted everything done exactly right and according to the rules. If a lady was supposed to ride sidesaddle, then Tall Joe's daughter must ride sidesaddle. Not on a man's saddle. Not ever. No questions.

Emma waited for Edward and Katherine. The three made their plans together.

Each day after that, Edward had both horses ready when Katherine arrived. She rode Nugget on the sidesaddle while he followed on Princess and the western saddle. They started down the little-used path that led to the field. Once out of sight, Edward dismounted and returned to his chores. Katherine waited there, in the woods, for Emma.

On returning, the two girls left Princess hidden and walked from the path's end to the barn, with Katherine leading Nugget. So long as no one was about, Edward set off along the path to collect Princess. And so the days slipped by.

———————————

Cool sunshine filtered through tall cedars, casting long shadows across the field. Emma took a deep breath of clean, crisp air and tapped Princess' sides, determined to get it right this time. For twenty feet, maybe more, she stayed with the horse as it joggled up and down. She felt comfortable, in tune with Princess' movements. Then she lost the rhythm, bounced helplessly, and reined Princess in, frustrated with herself.

Katherine pulled up beside her. "You're doing much better," she said, "but trotting takes time to master. I think it's the hardest part of learning to ride. Why don't you try a canter? It's so much smoother, it really is."

Emma shook her head. Katherine had suggested this before, but something held her back. A frightening image of herself, perched on the horse, racing along with such alarming speed it was impossible to stop. Impossible to remain in the saddle. "Trotting first. Once I master that, I can do anything."

Katherine pressed her lips together, her brow creased. She leaned forward to pat Liberty, then glanced back at Emma. "Suit yourself." She took off at a trot.

Emma watched her go. The girl might think she was better than Emma, but Katherine knew how to ride a horse, and that's for certain-sure. She was a good teacher too. For now, Emma needed Katherine and so was careful to do nothing that would make her cross enough to give up.

Such as call the horse Liberty. In her own mind, though, Emma always thought of it as Liberty. That's what the horse meant to her, and that was what she would name it.

Halfway around the field, Katherine urged Liberty into a canter. Emma had to admit, the ride did look a lot smoother, but even so...

She tapped Princess, and they resumed their slow plod around the field. Once around and Emma decided to try trotting again. This time it hurt. Her knee hurt. Her hip hurt. She was tired. But a walk was too easy. Too boring. She needed to do more. She took a deep breath, gathered her courage, and tapped the horse with both heels. Princess snorted, shook her head, and kept on trotting. Emma tapped a little harder, flicked the reins. "Go!" she cried. "Faster, Princess! Canter!" If there was any change in the horse's gait, it was to prance just a little higher and make Emma bounce a little harder with every step.

Hoofbeats, quick and hard, raced up behind her. Princess put her ears back and trotted a little faster. The hoofbeats came closer, thundering up behind them. Princess stretched out her neck, lengthened her stride, and picked up speed.

Emma opened her mouth, tried to cry out, but the sound jammed in her throat. Wind blew into her face. She flew over the ground at a speed no human was meant to go, and that's for certain-sure. Emma gripped the saddlehorn and clung to the horse with her knees. A moment later, she threw back her head and laughed. She was cantering! And she wasn't falling off. Katherine was right, this cantering was all smooth and easy, not like that horrid trotting business. Not at all.

Katherine pulled up beside her, slowing Nugget to keep pace. Emma was doing well, and Katherine smiled to see her. Princess had reacted just the way she hoped, breaking into a canter because she hated to be overtaken by the younger horse. Katherine ignored the little, niggling voice that reminded her Emma would soon be ready to ride Nugget.

"That was splendid!" Emma bubbled over with excitement as they rode back along the path in almost total darkness. "I can hardly wait for tomorrow! You were right, cantering is so much easier. I shall be ready to ride Liberty in no time!"

Katherine grimaced. Her hands twisted around the reins. Liberty. Well, she would need to get used to it, wouldn't she? Not Nugget. No more Nugget. Before long, it would be herself riding Princess and Emma getting used to Liberty, her own horse. Her throat ached. She leaned forward to pat Nugget's warm neck. "You'll always be Nugget to me," she whispered.

"Miss Harris!" The voice was so loud, so close in the darkness, Katherine almost tumbled from the saddle.

Nugget had stopped without being told. Katherine realized in an instant that, lost in her own concerns, she had strayed beyond the end of the path. She squinted, breathless, into the gloom ahead. The tall, shadowy figure of a man loomed in the clearing near the barn door.

"Mr. Bentley!" Katherine called, louder than necessary. "What a pleasant surprise!" She urged Nugget up the slope, so close the horse almost tromped on Mr. Bentley's toes. Behind him, Katherine caught a quick flicker of movement. On silent feet, a dark shape circled around them, vanishing against the background of dark woods.

"I stopped by to see how Emma is doing with her riding lessons," he explained. "Is she with you?" He leaned sideways in an attempt to see around Nugget.

"Emma is doing very well," Katherine told him. "She cantered for the first time today and is learning how to trot."

"I see you are riding the horse?"

"Yes. Well, I'm..."

"Katherine still needs to exercise Nugget," Emma said, emerging from the path on foot. "And sometimes I get tired from riding and prefer to walk home."

Katherine slid to the ground. She clutched Nugget's reins and began talking, saying anything to keep Mr. Bentley's attention away from the dark figure behind them. "Emma is learning quickly. Next week, I shall be going home for the Christmas holiday, but in the new year we'll soon have her ready and able to ride with you to that acreage you plan on pre-empting."

"I'm happy to hear it," Mr. Bentley said.

The three walked into the barn together, and Katherine led Nugget toward her stall. Behind them a horse snorted, hoofs struck the floor, heavy and slow. She turned to see Edward leading Princess through the door, her head low, a cloud of vapor rising from her nostrils.

"Good evening, sir," he said, "and ladies." He nodded politely. "I must have just missed you. I've had Princess out for her exercise, but she tires quickly these days, especially with all my weight on her back."

"I can imagine," Emma remarked, "the poor horse!"

Tall Joe laughed. "But not nearly so bad as your poor horse racing under the enormous bulk of Mayor Harris!"

While the men laughed, Emma turned to Katherine, embarrassed that Tall Joe made fun of Mayor Harris in front of her. To her surprise, Katherine was laughing too.

The next day, she got her chance to question Katherine. They were riding side by side at a slow pace, cooling the horses after a hard ride, when Katherine confirmed she would be leaving at the end of the week.

"I don't understand. How can you be going home for Christmas; doesn't your family live right here in Victoria?" Emma asked.

Katherine shook her head. "My family lives on a farm outside the small town of Hope, but right now my parents are running a store up in Yale. They say it is a favor to Mr. Roberts, who owns the store, but I know they're relieved not to spend an entire winter on the farm."

"Then Mayor Harris is not your father?"

"Mayor Harris? He's no relation at all."

"And you are not rich and spoiled?"

"Not so's I noticed." Katherine laughed. "The truth is, I thought you were the rich and spoiled one."

"Me?" Emma's head jerked toward Katherine. "Whatever gave you that idea?"

"Oh, I don't know. Could be the way you speak so precisely, as if you think I won't understand proper English. Could be the fact that you live with governor and Mrs. Douglas. Or it might even be that fancy ring of yours." Katherine's eyes wandered to Emma's hand, lightly holding Princess' reins.

Emma glanced down too. Today the ring was no more than a lump inside a warm glove, but she turned her hand away. She searched for something to say, some way to turn the subject away from herself as neatly as she had turned the ring. What happened next took her by surprise, as if something inside her gave way, a dark barrier crumbled to let light shine through. Hearing the truth about Katherine gave her the strength to be honest about herself. "If I speak carefully, it is because I am afraid of making mistakes," she explained. "I live with the Douglas family because I'm their housemaid, and," she drew a shaky breath, "my mother gave me this ring the night before she died. The ring once belonged to Tall Joe's grandmother."

Emma stopped there, thinking she had said too much already but, to her horror, words kept tumbling from her mouth as if she had lost all control over it. "Seems like Tall Joe took off with his cousin to seek his fortune. My mother begged to go along, but Tall Joe was that stubborn and said the gold fields were no place for a lady. He promised to send for her as soon as he struck it rich." Emma hesitated, then added, "But me mam never did hear from him again. An' it's only because of the ring he knew me once I got here on me own." Oh, Emma put a hand to her mouth, realizing she had spoken so fast her perfect English slipped away.

Katherine didn't appear to notice. "How dreadful for you! Small wonder you don't trust Tall Joe." She paused, her brow creased in thought. "So if you're just thirteen, Emma, that must mean Tall Joe ran off back in 1848 after hearing of the gold found at Sutter's Mill? I read all about the California Gold Rush in a book my teacher loaned me."

Emma nodded. She guessed Katherine was right – somewhere in California was all she knew of it. But she didn't trust herself to speak right now. No telling what words might come flying from her mouth, making her sound like the street urchin she really was. At least she could keep that a secret from Katherine.

They rode on, Nugget gradually outpacing the slower horse, each girl lost in her own thoughts, each needing time to absorb this new information. Emma chided herself for saying so much, for letting Katherine know she was a servant girl and a pauper. And how foolish could she be? She glared at Katherine's back. "Well, an' at least she doesn't know you're a brideship girl," Emma told herself. "Let that slip and she'll never speak to you again."

Nugget stopped, and Katherine twisted in the saddle to look back at Emma, her face pale. When she spoke, her voice sounded tortured, as if she felt the pain as deeply as Emma herself. "You must miss her so much!"

Emma nodded. Her eyes stung. The ring lay heavy on her finger.

Katherine waited for Princess to catch up and stop beside Nugget. "Emma," she said in a croaky voice, "there's something I want to show you."

Emma waited, but Katherine only sat stock-still on the horse, staring straight ahead as if looking at something that was never there at all. Emma sensed a battle going on in Katherine's mind, so she waited until at last Katherine reached into the pocket of her skirt and pulled out a small cloth bag. She opened the drawstring and turned the bag upside down, letting a large gold nugget fall onto her palm. She held it toward Emma.

"Do you see how it looks like a rose?"

Emma nodded again, blinking because her eyes had gone blurry. She was surprised to see tears in Katherine's eyes too.

"I always keep it with me," Katherine said. "My sister gave it to me before she died." Her voice dropped to the faintest of whispers. "I miss her too."

12

"Oh, look!" Katherine grabbed Mrs. Morris' arm. "There they are. See – there's Mother and Father, and...oh! George too. He's come to meet me!" Katherine let go of Mrs. Morris and waved both arms above her head, jumping up and down on the deck of the sternwheeler as it steamed into Hope.

Mrs. Morris brushed her arm where Katherine had held it. "Honestly," she placed a hand over her chest, "I never saw such a display from a lady!"

"Then I'm glad I'm not one!" Katherine replied, jumping a little higher and waving a little more frantically, more to annoy Mrs. Morris than anything else. Mother spotted her on the crowded deck and waved back, her arm raised high over her head. She grabbed her husband's arm and pointed. A huge smile spread over Father's face. He extended both arms toward Katherine as if to reach up and wrap her in a huge hug. Even George smiled up at her. With a quick wave, he hurried toward the riverbank.

"Well!" Mrs. Morris breathed. "Country life certainly does change some people!"

Yes, and for the better, Katherine thought, but didn't say, because Mrs. Morris was in a bad enough mood already. The woman had not wanted to leave Victoria and miss so many of the parties planned around the Christmas season. But there was no one else to accompany Katherine, and it was out of the question for a young, unmarried girl to travel without an adult. So Mrs. Morris had reluctantly agreed. "If I do not come with you, you will not be able to go at all," she told Katherine. "We would not want you missing Christmas with your family, now would we?"

"No, of course not." Katherine had held her tongue in order to appease Mrs. Morris. She knew the truth though. The widow did not want to be stuck with Katherine over Christmas, dragging her along to parties where Katherine would embarrass her by never managing to fit in. Better to take a quick trip up to Hope and get rid of the girl for two weeks than put up with her in Victoria.

The sternwheeler nudged up against shore and Katherine forgot all about Mrs. Morris as she ran to meet George, who was waiting to help her down. She reached for his hand and scrambled to the ground before the ramp could be set in place.

"I'm so happy to see you, George!"

The two climbed up the low bank, where Katherine found herself engulfed in hugs, first by her mother, then her father. "Your mother missed you desperately," Father said, squeezing her so hard she could scarcely breathe.

"I missed her too," Katherine said, "and you just as much."

He squeezed even tighter until Katherine gasped for air. She blinked, looking over his shoulder, blinked again and forgot about breathing altogether.

Not ten yards away stood a tall, strongly built young man dressed in work clothes similar to George's. His clear brown eyes held hers for a moment before he nodded and looked away. William. Katherine wanted to run over, tell him she was going to school in Victoria now and ask if he was doing well.

But Father turned her around with an arm resting on her shoulders. "We must go and greet Mrs. Morris," he said.

It was only then Katherine realized how heavily he leaned on her. She had almost forgotten about his injured leg. As they walked toward the bank with Mother on her other side, Katherine glanced back, but William had vanished into the milling crowd.

In spite of her joy at homecoming, a deep sadness settled over her. She had not seen William for so long and now, today, he was so very close, and yet she could not speak to him. She wondered why he was here and not with his family up in their village near Lytton.

"We have the wagon waiting." Father led the way, his hand pressing on Katherine's shoulder while Mother and Mrs. Morris followed close behind. "George is riding Duke back. He'll have the tea ready when we arrive."

George? Make tea? Katherine marveled at the thought.

She shivered and pulled her cloak closer as they walked across brittle brown grass near the Fraser. The ground was crunchy underfoot. A wind whisked down the valley, carrying a bite much fiercer than anything in Victoria. Black clouds hung low and threatening over the mountains. "It looks like snow," her father said. "We must hurry back."

"Don't tell him I said so," Mother added, "but your brother is excited about showing you all the work he has done since you left."

Katherine opened her mouth to ask what horse might

be pulling the wagon if George was riding Duke, but was interrupted by Mrs. Morris' high-pitched complaint.

"So that is why you're forcing me to spend a night in the wilderness?"

"We don't mean to force you, Isabelle," Mother said. "And we're very grateful you agreed to accompany Katherine home. But as the boat doesn't return to Victoria until tomorrow, there isn't a great deal of choice."

"We could find lodging for you here in Hope if you would prefer," Katherine suggested.

Father's grip on her shoulder tightened, not quite hurting, but close enough. She said nothing more.

Mrs. Morris may have muttered a reply, but Katherine didn't hear because right then the wagon came into view, a familiar black horse hitched to it. "Coal!" she cried without thinking.

Father stopped abruptly. "How do you know the horse's name?"

She noticed William then, standing beside the wagon, waiting to help them climb aboard. Katherine was so surprised she could scarcely think. "I, uh, I don't know. He's so black, I guess, he reminds me of coal."

Her father looked skeptical. "But that's..."

"William here has been helping George around the farm," Mother interrupted. "Wait until you see the barn they're building. It's almost finished, and the well is too! And they've worked on the cabin – you'll be amazed, Katherine. William is a wonderful influence on George. He is such a hard worker."

At this, Mrs. Morris gave a loud *Humph*. She stood back with her arms folded across her drooping chest and refused to let William hand her up into the wagon. As a result,

Father had to step forward to help her and Katherine stood on his other side to prevent him from falling.

It took both William and Katherine to help Father up into the seat, and then William turned to Katherine. His hand felt warm and strong as it closed around hers. A tingle of happiness surged through her body. She glanced up at him shyly.

He stared down at her, as stern as the last time she saw him – that day at his village with his father looking on, when William told her a man could not be friends with a girl.

She let go of his hand and scrambled up to the seat on her own.

"It certainly is cold enough in this godforsaken country," Mrs. Morris complained as they bounced along the frozen road toward the Harris farm. She sat beside Mother, sharing a warm blanket, their backs to William, who occupied the small driver's seat at the front. Katherine and her father sat opposite the two women, facing forward, a second blanket over their knees. "And it is such a long way from civilization."

The wheels dipped into a particularly deep pothole. "Ugh," Mrs. Morris moaned, "this is a horrid, rough ride." She placed a gloved hand on Mother's arm. "You must be a saint to cope with all of this, my dear."

"It's not so bad once you get used to it," Mother replied. "But I must admit, we do enjoy living in Yale, where we have a little company."

"Yes, but you are so far from Society," Mrs. Morris sympathized. "And," she glanced over her shoulder at William, then leaned closer to Mother but didn't bother to lower her voice, "it is impossible to get any decent sort of help!"

Katherine could tell how angry William was by the way he held his shoulders, all hunched up and stiff. She leaned forward, intending to say a few choice words to Mrs. Morris, but Father pulled her back.

"We make do quite nicely," Mother said. "And without William's help and others like him, many of us settlers would not survive in this wild colony. I don't expect our George would have accomplished half so much if William had not shown up to offer his services."

Katherine wondered exactly when William had arrived. She must have just missed him when she set out for Victoria. Did he only show up because he knew she had gone?

William deposited everyone at the cabin's front door and headed for the sturdy little barn to take care of the horses. Katherine watched him go. He and George had certainly done a splendid job on building the barn. More a large shed really, set not far from the house, its roof steeply pitched to prevent snow from accumulating. The wood-plank walls were finished and a wide door set in place. She started toward it, but George appeared at the cabin door just then.

"Tea's ready!" he announced.

Katherine stopped in the doorway. She could scarcely believe what she saw. There was fresh bread on the table, sourdough to be sure, but bread nevertheless. There was cheese and butter, blackberry jam and a big pot of tea, with the table neatly set. Behind the table, instead of the little lean-to kitchen and cramped room beside it where George slept, there was now a real, built-in kitchen and a proper bedroom. She hurried to inspect them.

The bedroom was scarcely large enough for a bed but

had an actual door and in the far wall a small, square window. The walls had no cracks between logs to let in the frigid winter wind. There was a proper roof above it and over the kitchen too, not one that looked about to collapse under the weight of the first snowfall.

"This is unbelievable! You've done so much."

"I couldn't have done it without William," George admitted as they rejoined the others.

Mrs. Morris clucked her tongue and lowered herself onto their one decent chair. It was Father's, who needed the comfort of it since his injury. But he said nothing and settled on one of the crude blocks of wood.

After tea, Father pushed himself up from the table. "I believe I shall take the newspapers Mrs. Morris so kindly brought along and read them in the bedroom, out of everyone's way."

Katherine smiled to herself, knowing he could not abide another minute in Mrs. Morris's company. Likely he would be snoring within five minutes.

"Well, I'm off to the barn," George said. "There's work to be done before we leave for Yale tomorrow."

Mother and Mrs. Morris remained at the table to catch up on news of Victoria while Katherine cleared the table and washed the dishes. That done, she bundled into warm clothes and hurried outside.

Tiny, dry pellets of snow floated from a slate-grey sky as Katherine scurried toward the new barn. Inside there was room enough for four stalls, a small storage area, and a loft overflowing with sweet-smelling hay. Duke and Coal took up two of the stalls while their milk cow, Genevieve, watched Katherine lazily from a third. George was busy hammering boards to complete a wall of the storage area.

"You've done a splendid job here too," Katherine said. "And in such a short time. I still can't believe it!"

George spoke around a mouthful of nails that altered the sounds of his words. "Isn't this why you dragged me home?"

Katherine smiled. "I wasn't certain you would actually do anything. You didn't accomplish much last summer!"

George spit the nails into his hand. "Yes, well, it's not easy to work with Father standing over me explaining what I'm doing wrong every minute."

"I know!" Katherine laughed briefly, but something else occupied her mind. Should she ask? No... Yes... Now or never. "Did William arrive when Father was still here?"

"No, he showed up after they left. He needed work because there weren't enough salmon caught in the river to last his people until spring. He blames the shortage on the construction of the wagon road."

"Oh, but George, do you think that could be true?"

Her brother shrugged. "I have no idea. At any rate, we pay him what we can, mostly in food Mother sends from the store up to his family's winter village."

"That's good then," Katherine said.

"Wait until you see the well! William's out there now. We had hoped to finish it before you got here as a surprise, since you were the one who complained so much about it."

"I was the one who had to fetch water in that contraption you and Father built!" she pointed out. George didn't answer but stuffed the nails back into this mouth.

"I guess I shall go have a look at the well then."

George nodded, already back at his task.

Katherine spotted William working on the framework above the well. He didn't see her coming, and she chuckled to herself, remembering the day she first met William. She had been leaning over the riverbank, using a long pole and a pulley system rigged up by Father and George to haul up a bucket of water.

Hey! William had called, so close behind she had dropped the pole over the bank. Today, she would get even.

"Hey!" she cried out, stifling a laugh.

He swung around, the look on his face so fierce she jumped back.

"Never creep up on a man that way!"

"I didn't creep, I only walked. Can I help it if you didn't hear me?"

William turned his back and continued working. Of course he wouldn't think it was funny. Why should he? Too late, Katherine remembered how cross she had been at him. Even so, he didn't need to yell at her. He didn't need to turn away and pretend she wasn't even here. "That's what you did to me when I was fetching water that day," she reminded him.

Still he didn't answer.

"You're doing an excellent job," she said.

He acted as if he did not hear.

"Thank you for helping George. He could never have accomplished half so much by himself."

No reply.

"William?" Maybe he wasn't interested. Maybe he didn't care. But William was the only person who had really listened to her after Susan died, and she missed his company. She needed to confide in him now, whether he liked it or not. "I'm learning a lot at school, but I haven't made any friends. No one likes me except for the little ones. The only girl in the whole town who speaks to me is Emma Curtis, and she doesn't even go to school. But guess what?" Katherine realized she was babbling. She forced herself into silence. Perhaps curiosity would get the better of him. Perhaps not.

She waited. She put out her hand, palm upward, watching tiny grains of snow land and melt away in the warmth of her skin. It seemed William was too busy to talk to her. She turned to go.

"What?"

"Oh, William, I found Nugget!" She smiled up at him. "She belongs to Emma, who wants to call her Liberty, which is a stupid name. But luckily for me, Emma doesn't know how to ride, so I'm teaching her. That means I get to ride Nugget every day."

"It is good you have a friend. This is what you wanted most of all."

"I did. But Emma's not really my friend, she's...well, she's just Emma."

"Then you must learn to be a friend to her," William said. "Katherine, our fathers are right about us. We cannot be friends. Our worlds are too far apart."

"Oh!" What was he saying? Katherine bit her lip.

"Next summer I will marry – a young woman from a nearby village."

"Oh!" she said again. "Oh, but..."

"She will be a good wife for me."

"All right then." Katherine knew this was true, the way it must be – she had known it all along, really. But seeing William again like this made her remember how much she had liked him. How he had been a friend to her when she felt so alone. "Congratulations. I'm certain you will be very happy." She turned away because her eyes began to water.

"Katherine?" William stepped closer.

She focused on the toes of her boots, on little white pellets landing on them. A skiff of white covered the ground at her feet. William placed his fingertips under her chin and raised it until she was forced to look up at him.

"It's the cold wind," she explained. "It makes my eyes water. I'm not used to the cold, you see, in Victoria..."

"You also will be happy in your life," he interrupted. "This is good."

"Yes." She gulped and pulled away. She darted back to the cabin, her head down against a rising wind.

Six inches of snow covered the ground, and brittle stars hung in a cold black sky the next morning when everyone crowded into the wagon to which George and William had affixed runners. They pulled into Hope with a pale sun struggling to sweep away the stars.

Black smoke billowed into the sky from the sternwheeler's smokestack, showing that the crew were pouring on coal to build a full head of steam before tackling the rapids. A blast of the horn echoed through the crisp air.

"Hurry," Father said, "or we'll be left behind."

In the rush to climb aboard, Katherine didn't get a chance to say goodbye to William, and when she looked back from the deck he had disappeared. She realized, too late, that she hadn't apologized for Mrs. Morris' rudeness.

On reaching Yale, passengers disembarked and supplies bound for the general store were unloaded quickly so the boat could head back downriver. They said their goodbyes to Mrs. Morris while still on board.

"Well, I can't say I'll miss her," Father remarked as the boat pulled away.

"Is she like that all the time?" George asked.

"She's usually kept busy in Victoria," Katherine said. "So I don't see too much of her."

"Luckily for you." George bent to pick up a parcel destined for the store while their parents hurried ahead to open the doors.

Christmas morning, George and Katherine followed their parents, boots crunching over new-fallen snow, up a small rise to a little white church tucked at the base of steep mountains. The lower slopes, stripped barren in the building of Yale, might be ugly come spring, but today they sparkled pure white under a fresh blanket of snow.

Their parents clung to one another, arm in arm, their heads bowed. Katherine knew they were thinking of other Christmases. They were thinking of Susan. She glanced at her brother, but he refused to look her way. He grunted as if in pain, his breath rising into the crisp air.

"Oh, George," she whispered, slipping her hand through his bent arm. She could say nothing more. Nothing more was needed. George patted her hand. Her eyes stung.

It seemed the entire town was gathered in the church. And after the service almost everyone remained to chat in the warmth of the room.

"How are you enjoying school in Victoria?" asked a young mother with a baby in her arms, a child clutching her hand and another clinging to her long skirt.

"Very much," Katherine replied. "I'm learning a lot and I always enjoy helping the little ones with their schoolwork."

"Oh, if only someone here in Yale would do that! I try to teach my children at home, but there is so little time, what with washing and cooking and growing food and caring for the youngest ones."

"Yes, it must be difficult to do everything yourself." Katherine watched a group of children, eight or nine of them, chasing one another about the room while their mothers tried in vain to get them to settle down. She thought of the plans she and Susan had shared. The dream of starting a school.

The rich aroma of slow-roasting goose wafted out to greet them as the family approached their comfortable living quarters behind the store. Hungry, they hurried inside. It was mid afternoon of the following day when townspeople began dropping by. The women brought warm pies and cakes, while some of the men carried whiskey bottles tucked in their pockets. The women and children remained in the kitchen while the men, including George, wandered into the small parlour. Other than Katherine and George, everyone was either an adult or a child under ten.

After serving coffee and passing around a plate of food, Katherine wandered aimlessly through the crowded room, too young to chat with the women, too old to play with the children. She paused at the woodstove and raised both hands to its warmth.

"Can you read?"

Seated on a braided rug, a small girl balanced a heavy

book on her knees. Katherine recognized her as the one clutching her mother's hand at church the day before.

"I got this book from my grandmother. She lives a long ways away in Scotland."

"Would you like me to read you a story?"

The child nodded.

"Good then." Happy for the company, Katherine settled beside the little girl and started reading. But the story was long and preachy and threatened to put both of them to sleep. Closing the book, Katherine began to relate one of her favorite stories from childhood. Other children began to gather around her, sitting on the rug near the stove.

"I have a book too," said one of the boys, holding it up. "But it's hard to read by myself."

"Then let's read it together," Katherine suggested. The boy sat beside her, reading aloud, while she helped him over the difficult parts.

"Can we come back soon?" he asked his mother as they left.

Katherine smiled to hear it.

The following day was a quiet one. Snow fell steadily, making walking difficult. The store was open but not as busy as usual. At this time of year it did a good enough business with local folk, but come spring the store would be bustling once more with miners purchasing supplies before heading up the Cariboo Road to seek their fortunes.

Katherine settled in the parlour to read, but the book didn't hold her interest, and she grew restless. She stood and went to the window. Snow fell so heavily it obliterated the river directly across the road. She decided against a walk. What was there to do? She wandered down the short hallway and paused at a closed door. She knew it led to the attic and wondered what treasures might be stored up there. Perhaps there were books just waiting to be read.

The door creaked open on a dimly lit stairway. She followed the dusty stairs to a long, rectangular room. The steeply gabled roof sloped to meet the floor along each side. At each end, a small window offered light enough to see. She paused beneath the ridge and surveyed a large, empty space high enough to for an adult to stand in comfortably.

Katherine hugged her arms around herself in the quiet cold. She thought of the children here who couldn't read their new Christmas books. She pictured little desks around her. Shelves lined with books. Lanterns hanging from beams overhead. She shivered. A woodstove for warmth. She hurried back down the stairs, closed the door, and wandered back to the parlour, deep in thought.

The night before returning to Victoria, Katherine could think of little else but Nugget. If all went well, she and Mother would arrive safely in Victoria by the following evening. The day after that, she would see Nugget again. And Emma of course. Katherine was surprised to realize she looked forward to seeing Emma as much as Nugget.

"This has been a good Christmas," Mother said, packing her bags to accompany Katherine. "Better than I could have expected – without Susan."

Katherine nodded. Her eyes misted, thinking of her sister, but for Mother's sake she managed a smile. "It was fun having so many people to visit."

Mother folded her nightdress. "I shall be sorry when

Mr. Roberts comes home in spring and we need to return to the farm. More so now that your father has finally realized farming is not for us."

"I wonder..." Katherine said, picking up a book of Mr. Brett's and placing it with her packed clothing. "Mother, I have an idea. Do you think it would be all right if I wrote a letter to Mr. Roberts?"

"Whatever for?"

"I'd rather not say just yet, but there may be a solution to make everyone happy. Could you please give me his address in Jamaica?"

Mother looked undecided.

"Just one letter, Mother. I will let you know if anything comes of it. I promise."

Her mother put down the blouse she was folding. She glanced toward the parlour, where Father was reading by the fire. Then she walked over to her writing desk and retrieved the address.

13

Emma pushed open the gate and followed the gravel path to Mrs. Morris' front door. Wind whistled around the corners of the small house. A strong gust whooshed up from behind, speeding her along. Her stomach ached almost as bad as back in Manchester where she went days without a scrap of food and nothing but mud-brown water to drink. This pain, though, was not due to hunger. It was brought on by fear.

She should never have come here, even if Katherine did tell her mother about Emma being a housemaid and all, and Mrs. Harris didn't mind. Neither of them suspected she was a brideship girl. Who didn't look down on brideship girls, she'd like to know? Paying passengers thought them no more than *living freight*, and didn't the townsfolk line the streets to mock the girls that first day off the ship?

She stared at the closed door. "This will be somethin' 'orrible," she muttered. "Imagine me, Emma Curtis, gettin' meself invited to tea at a proper toffken." She turned away, into the wind, ready to run off. Her cloak flapped around her like a great sail, and she grabbed at it. Her eyes fell on the opal ring. Would Mama be proud of her now?

The door swung inward. Emma stopped breathing.

What if it was that Mrs. Morris just now leaving her house?

"Emma! I saw you on the walk, but you took so long to reach the door I couldn't wait. Come in, it's cold out there! My mother is eager to meet you, I've told her all about you."

Emma's stomach twisted. Not all, she thought. Not half. And if the truth came out, not one of them would speak to her ever again. Even Katherine would be shocked.

Katherine took Emma's cloak and hung it on a tall wooden stand. Then she led Emma into the parlour, a small, gloomy room cluttered with furniture. A woman sat in a stuffed armchair, stitching a dress draped over her lap. Her hair, in the soft lamplight, shone pale gold. Seeing Emma, the woman set aside the dress and stood up.

"Mother, this is my, uh – my friend, Emma Curtis. Emma, my mother, Mrs. Harris."

Emma stared in surprise. She knew this woman was older than Emma's own mother had been. And yet she moved with such grace, the knuckles of her hands were not swollen and sore, and her face was scarcely lined. And how those blue eyes sparkled. She still looked pretty, even at her great age! Mrs. Harris smiled and revealed a row of strong teeth, not one of them missing. "It's lovely to meet you at last, Emma. How do you do?"

"It is a pleasure to meet you too," Emma managed to say. Her voice sounded strangled and the beat of her heart pumped loud in her ears.

"Please, sit down. Katherine will fetch the tea as it's the cook's afternoon off."

Emma perched on the very edge of an upholstered chair. She was an impostor, she should never have come. Katherine gave her an odd look, as if wondering why

Emma was acting so strangely. Then she turned and left the room.

"Katherine hasn't told me where you are from, Emma. Did you grow up in England?"

"I...yes." Wind screamed around the windows. Emma listened for a harsh footstep, afraid Mrs. Morris might be at home. Emma had encountered that woman once before and, like as not, she would recognize Emma.

"And what part of England would that be, if you don't mind my asking?"

Emma did mind, but she had no idea how to change the subject. "The north," she said, hoping to leave it at that. But when Mrs. Harris said nothing and only waited, Emma added, "Manchester."

"Oh yes, the manufacturing town."

Emma nodded, wishing she could leave now.

"I understand thousands of paupers live on the streets of Manchester."

"They have no other choice."

Mrs. Harris glanced up, studied Emma for a moment, and returned to her stitching. "Katherine tells me you're learning to ride?"

"Oh, yes!" Emma replied, grateful to be on safer ground. She spoke carefully, testing each word before speaking it aloud. "I am enjoying it immensely! Katherine is an excellent teacher."

"I expect she is. Tell me, what is it your father did in Manchester?"

Uh. What to say? "My father," she said, fumbling for words. Just in time, Emma remembered that Tall Joe had asked her to convey his regrets. "My father was very disappointed that he could not join us today but he and his cousin are meeting with Governor Douglas to inquire about pre-empting some land for a farm."

"Yes. He sent me a note this morning. How unfortunate. And Mrs. Morris has left for a previous engagement, but I think Katherine mentioned our hostess was busy today?"

"Yes," Emma's shoulders relaxed. "Unfortunate indeed."

Katherine burst into the room, carrying a tray with teapot, cups, saucers, cream and sugar, various sandwiches cut into tiny sections, and squares of little cakes. "If you want my opinion," she said, "it's not unfortunate at all. We were quite glad to be rid of her."

"Katherine!" her mother scolded. "That is no way to speak of our hostess!"

"I'm sorry, Mother," Katherine said, and winked at Emma. "Even if it is true."

Mrs. Harris shook her head sadly.

After that, things went much more smoothly. They discussed Victoria and Hope and the huge differences between the two communities. In the one, townsfolk liked to pretend they still lived in Britain, with all its strict rules of behavior and firm division between upper and lower classes. In the other, everyone worked hard simply to stay alive and had no time to fuss about rules that held no meaning for them.

They talked about farm life too. "It won't be easy for you," Mrs. Harris warned Emma, "not when you're used to an easier life."

Easy? Her life? Just then, taking a sip of tea with the cup held daintily by its delicate handle, her little finger curled perfectly, and trying her best to look ladylike,

Emma choked. She tried but couldn't stop coughing.

"Are you all right?" Mrs. Harris put down her cup and saucer and hurried over.

"Katherine, run and fetch a glass of water."

"I am so sorry," Emma gasped when she was able to speak. She accepted the glass from Katherine and took a small sip. She was mortified, she had tried so hard to be on her best behavior.

"That's perfectly all right," Mrs. Harris assured her. "It could happen to anyone."

"I'm sorry if we frightened you, telling you what hard work there is on a farm," Katherine said.

"I think I will like it," Emma told them. "My mother grew up in the countryside and always wanted to live away from the city."

"Well, you must be certain to tell your father you will need help," Mrs. Harris said. "What with three men to cook for and clean up after as well as all the farm chores that fall to us women."

Me have a girl helping out? And what would Mama think of that? Emma almost smiled. She was glad she came after all. Katherine's mother seemed kind enough, and these little cakes were delicious. She reached for another.

Then it happened.

The front door flew open along with a gust of wind. In walked a woman Emma recognized immediately. If there had been more than a drop of tea left in her cup, she would have spilled it, her hand shook that badly. Emma held the saucer with one hand and steadied the cup with the other, afraid it would shake right off and crash to the floor. She averted her face.

"Mrs. Morris," Mrs. Harris said, rising to her feet.

Katherine stood up too, and Emma followed suit. She kept her head bowed, staring into the teacup clutched against her stomach. With any luck Mrs. Morris would not recognize her.

Mrs. Harris went on. "I'm so pleased you arrived home in time to meet Katherine's friend, Emma Curtis. Emma, this is..."

"You!" Mrs. Morris raised her gloved hand and pointed a trembling finger at Emma. "In my home! If I had known it was you...well, I never!" She turned to Mrs. Harris. "This is the very girl I told you about," she sputtered, "the one who dared to insult my very good friend, Mrs. Steeves, whom I introduced you to only yesterday!"

Katherine narrowed her eyes. She happened to know Mrs. Steeves was about as pleasant a person as Mrs. Morris herself. "Whatever Emma said, I'm certain Mrs. Steeves must have deserved it," she said.

A deathly silence settled over the small room. Emma continued to stare into her teacup, trembling on its saucer. Katherine glared at Mrs. Morris. Mrs. Morris appealed to Mrs. Harris. Mrs. Harris frowned at her daughter.

"Do you see what I'm expected to put up with? Your daughter has no respect for me whatsoever!" Mrs. Morris whined.

"Katherine!" her mother said. "That is entirely unacceptable behavior. You must apologize at once."

But Katherine was too angry to speak. This woman was unendurable. She would never apologize, no matter what her mother said.

"And to think," Mrs. Morris sputtered, "to think your daughter had the nerve to invite one of those dreadful *Tynemouth* wretches into my home. My home!" She pressed the back of her hand against her forehead. "Oh! It's all coming back to me now. The girl is a cripple no less. A cripple and a brideship girl who works for that dreadful woman Governor Douglas chose to marry!"

At this, Mrs. Harris went white and her eyes blazed. "A cripple, because she limps slightly? I suppose you call my husband a cripple too, behind his back. And there's no need to insult Mrs. Douglas either. She seems to me a good woman even if she is not British."

She glanced over at Katherine. "I will admit Katherine has been unforgivably rude, but Emma here..." She broke off and turned to the spot where Emma had been standing a moment before. It was empty. "You've frightened her off, the poor child!"

"Good riddance is all I can say!"

"And I'll tell you what I say..." Katherine began, but her mother cut in.

"You are dismissed."

"But..."

"Katherine, go to your room immediately. I shall deal with you later. Mrs. Morris and I have matters to discuss."

Katherine stomped out of the parlour. She ran up the narrow staircase, slammed the door to her room, locked it with the key, and plopped herself down on the edge of the bed. Board money or not, Mrs. Morris would kick her out now and Katherine would have to return home with her mother. No more school, no more Nugget, no more friend.

Emma had never once mentioned being from the brideship, *Tynemouth*. If she had, would things have turned out differently? Would Katherine have confided in her mother? Would they have invited Emma for tea had they known? Katherine couldn't say for sure. One thing was clear though. Emma still didn't trust her.

———————

Well and what a fool she had been, Emma told herself over and over as she scurried away from Mrs. Morris' house, her head bowed against wind-driven rain. She should never have gone. What's more, she should never have started to like Katherine. Get close to someone and they died on you or sent you away, one of the two, and shame on her for forgetting it.

Emma saw the horrified look on Katherine's face as she listened to Mrs. Morris' vicious words. And Mrs. Harris too looked mortified to learn she had invited a bride-ship girl to take tea with them. One of those half-starved orphans plucked from the streets and workhouses of England. Up to no good, an' that's for certain-sure.

She kept her head down, fighting tears. Her leg ached and she limped badly but didn't care who noticed. She started across the James Bay Bridge. Battered by high winds off the harbour, the bridge deck trembled beneath her feet. A strong gust whipped up and tossed Emma hard against the railing. She regained her footing and hunched into the wind, clutching her cloak close while rain pelted her face so hard it hurt. Out of nowhere, a strong arm slipped across her back, a solid body came between her and the wind. She glanced up.

"Oh, Edward, you frightened me!"

"Didn't mean to. I saw you fighting the wind and thought you could use some help." He kept walking as he spoke. Helping her along with him, he shielded her from the full force of the wind. A little thrill shivered through Emma. Edward was such a comfort. And he fancied her, she was certain of that. She smiled at him.

"You're still too thin, Emma. That's why you get so cold and the wind knocks you over like a twig. You need some meat on your bones, like Katherine."

Katherine? Emma stopped. They were almost across the bridge where the wind's fury lessened. "I don't need anyone's help, thank you very much," she snapped.

Edward's eyes crinkled with concern. "You're not crying, Emma?"

" 'Course not. It's the rain and salt spray and nothing more!" She walked away, but Edward kept pace, his hand at her elbow.

"I'll thank you to take your hand away and leave me be."

He let go.

Will you never learn, you foolish girl? Emma chided herself as she continued toward the Douglas house alone. Her cheeks burned. Of course Edward didn't fancy her, not since that Katherine came along. Katherine, who rode a horse so perfectly well. Katherine, who looked so lovely and wasn't all skin and bone. When spring came round and it was time for Edward to leave Beckley Farm and go as hired hand with Tall Joe, Ned Turner, and herself to help get their farm started, Edward would change his mind, and that's for certain-sure. He would never want to leave his precious Katherine behind.

Emma let herself in as quietly as possible with the wind trying to fling the door from its hinges. She tiptoed up to her room. She didn't need any questions from Mrs. Douglas right now.

Katherine sat on her bed, seething with anger. By flickering candlelight she attempted to read *Oliver Twist*, one of the books Mr. Brett had lent her. But Charles Dickens exaggerated so – England was not half so bad as he made out. There were workhouses to care for homeless people, and no human being could be half so cruel as all those people were to poor Oliver. She put down the book and leaned back on her pillow.

What had Emma's life been like before coming here? If it were anywhere near as bad as Oliver's, then small wonder she chose not to talk about it. But of course it couldn't have been. Help was always there for poor children. Wasn't it?

A powerful gust howled around her window. Rain beat against the glass. Katherine shuddered. Her mother and Mrs. Morris must be talking up a storm of their own in the parlour below.

The longer she waited, the angrier she grew. How could they sit down there and blame an innocent girl for all the troubles that happened to her, as if Emma had brought them on herself? Katherine got up and strode to the door. She would march downstairs and give them her opinion, like it or not. Her hand was on the key when a knock on the door made her jump.

"Katherine! Let me in, I must talk to you!"

She unlocked the door.

Mother bustled in and shut the door behind her. "I've managed to settle things with Mrs. Morris," she whispered. She ushered her daughter over to the bed and sat beside her. "She's very upset, of course. You should never have spoken to her that way."

"But Mother, she was so rude!" Katherine's voice grew louder with each word. "And if you've met Mrs. Steeves, then you know she's a..."

Her mother's hand clapped over Katherine's mouth.

"Mrs. Steeves is a respected member of this community," Mother said. "Children must never be rude to adults. It is inexcusable!"

"Even if the adults are wrong?" Katherine asked.

"Unquestionably." Mother paused to think. "Katie, try to look at it this way. If you insult Mrs. Steeves, who is Mrs. Morris' good friend, then Mrs. Morris will naturally defend her, just as you defended Emma – in spite of everything."

Katherine started to object, but her mother went on. "In any event, it took some doing, but I managed to persuade Mrs. Morris to let you remain for the school term. I suspect she does not want to give up her board money. However, there are two conditions." She took a quick breath. "First, you must apologize," Mother put up her hand to silence Katherine, "and second, you must not continue this friendship with Emma."

"I can't do that," Katherine said flatly. "Not either of those things."

"I was afraid of that." Mother pressed her knuckles against her lips, thinking. "All right then, listen carefully. As for the apology, if you could merely say you're sorry for speaking back to her – without mentioning that she deserved it – I'm certain that would suffice."

Katherine didn't answer. How could she make her mother understand? She would never apologize after the way Mrs. Morris behaved.

"Could you do that, Katie? Otherwise you will need to return to Yale with me come Saturday."

Yale. A return to Yale now meant a return to the farm come spring. And Katherine was not ready to leave Victoria, not yet. By June, if she worked hard and with Mr. Brett's help, she would be ready to open a school for young students. And she couldn't bear to say goodbye to Nugget, not until she absolutely had to.

As for Emma? Katherine clung to the hope that her plan would work out for the best. That Mr. Roberts would want to sell his Yale properties to Father. In turn, if Father sold his farm to Mr. Bentley he should have enough money. Everyone would get what they wanted. Emma would live not too far away, and so would Nugget. Katherine eagerly awaited Mr. Roberts' reply to her letter – exactly how long would it take to reach Jamaica and for a reply to arrive in Victoria? She had no idea.

"Mother, I can apologize for talking back to Mrs. Morris, but how can I stop being friends with Emma?"

Mother placed her hand over Katherine's. "Katie dear, I'm not sure a brideship girl is suitable company for you. Can you not make friends with girls in your school?"

"No. Mother, I'm sorry, but those girls are as rude and pretentious as Mrs. Morris. And it's not Emma's fault there was no one in England to take care of her and she ended up on the *Tynemouth.*"

"The girl has a father here."

"Yes, but he left England before she was born! He didn't even know Emma when she arrived here, and then only because he recognized the ring on her finger. You see, it was the very ring he gave Emma's mother before he left. So it's Mr. Bentley's fault Emma is so alone in the world, not hers. Why should Emma take all the blame?"

"Katherine, I'm not so hard hearted as you think."

Katherine made a noise in her throat.

"Believe it or not, I've had my eyes opened since moving to British Columbia. I understand now, how easily one can run into difficulty through no fault of one's own."

"Then..."

"Katie, listen carefully. What Mrs. Morris and I agreed upon, specifically, is that you must not be seen in Victoria with Emma."

Katherine let her mother's words sink in.

14

Katherine hurried to Beckley Farm after school, planning exactly what she would say to Emma. First she would apologize for Mrs. Morris' inexcusable behavior. Then she would explain that it didn't matter to her, or her mother either, if Emma arrived here on the brideship. Katherine wanted to be Emma's friend and friends should never be afraid to tell each other the truth.

The warm, biting scent of hay and horses and manure welcomed her as she stepped into the barn. Neither horse was saddled, so Katherine set about getting them ready. Then she waited. She led Nugget outside, followed by Princess, and tied each horse to a fence rail. She waited some more.

The air was clear and crisp, the sky a cloudless blue. Katherine could hardly wait to set out; the days were short enough in January without getting a late start. She walked back through the barn and stood at the door looking out, expecting Emma to come limping into sight at any minute.

The shadows lengthened, Nugget stamped her feet and snorted, but still Emma did not show up. Something must have happened to delay her. If Katherine was going to ride at all today, she had to go now. She left Princess for Emma to ride and trotted off on Nugget.

Darkness had closed in when she returned and saw Princess still tied to the fence. Where was Emma? Katherine was grooming Nugget when she heard a soft footstep. At last! "Where have you been? You've missed today's ride altogether."

There was no reply. Katherine turned to see Mr. Bentley scowling down at her. "I've come to see my daughter," he said.

"Oh. Emma didn't show up for her ride today."

"That's odd," he scratched his beard, "because she told me only two days ago she would be here. I had planned to come watch her ride but got delayed."

"I see." That was it then. Emma must have suspected, and that was why she stayed away.

"Emma said she was learning to ride on Princess."

A chill ran down Katherine's spine, her mind raced. "Yes."

"And yet you have a man's saddle on the horse."

"Yes. You see...when I realized Emma was not coming, I thought Edward would exercise Princess, since the horse hasn't been out for two days. But I expect Edward is busy with other chores, so I shall remove the saddle now."

Mr. Bentley lifted up on his toes and back down. "All right then, I'll be over to the Douglas house and see that Emma is all right."

Again, the following day, no one was there when Katherine arrived. Neither horse was saddled.

"Oh, Nugget," Katherine whispered as she prepared for a ride, "I hope that awful incident with Mrs. Morris hasn't frightened Emma off. That girl is as touchy as they come." She sighed. "I guess we'll go without her again today." She led Nugget toward the barn door.

There was a soft footstep behind her. Katherine stopped and looked back. "Emma? Is that you? I was afraid you weren't coming."

Emma lurked in the shadows, her head down, eyes fixed on Nugget's hind legs. "I didn't want to," she admitted, her voice small. "I thought you wouldn't want to see me ever again. But Mrs. Douglas said I was wrong. She thinks I'm afraid and..." Emma looked up, "...could be she's right."

"What are you afraid of, Emma?" When Emma didn't reply, Katherine added, "Surely not of me?"

"I thought you wouldn't want anything more to do with me now that you know the truth."

"What truth? That you insulted Mrs. Steeves in some way? Believe me, I've met that woman and I'd insult her myself if I thought I could get away with it. Tell me, what happened?"

"I ran into those two, Mrs. Morris and Mrs. Steeves, one day and they called me a poor wretch from the *Tynemouth*."

Katherine nodded. "Those two think they're better than anyone."

"They do, but that isn't what got me so angry. It was when Mrs. Steeves insulted Mrs. Douglas and said the governor should have married a well-bred English lady that I called her a snob."

"Well then, Mrs. Steeves deserved it, just as I said."

Emma hadn't moved. She rubbed her hands together as if unsure what to do with them. "I never told you before, about how I arrived here. I didn't want you to know and now you've found out from Mrs. Morris, and your mother knows too."

"Knows what? That you arrived here on a brideship? Why should I care about that, Emma? I only wish you had trusted me enough to tell me."

"But..." Emma took a small step forward. "Katherine, don't you know how all the proper ladies turn their noses up on us brideship girls? Your mother will think I'm a bad influence and forbid you to be seen with me."

Katherine opened her mouth to object. Snapped it shut again. Wasn't that exactly what her mother said? "Emma, my mother might have felt that way once, but she's changed with everything that's happened this past year. I really think she's embarrassed by the way Mrs. Morris and her friends behave. At any rate, Mother is learning to see the value in all sorts of folk. So let's go riding and forget what everyone else thinks."

As January days lengthened into an unusually mild, dry February, Emma's riding ability improved steadily. She was ready to ride Nugget. They made the switch at the field, after the horse had released some of her energy with a good gallop.

"She's your horse now." Katherine bit her lip and avoided Emma's eyes. "You've got to practice riding her." She took a shaky breath. "And we had better start calling her by her new name too, so she can get used to it." Katherine turned to the horse. "Liberty!" she said, or tried to, but her voice cracked. She couldn't speak.

For months, Emma had waited for this moment, the day she could call her horse by the name she chose, the name that had meaning for herself alone. But now she saw Katherine's face and her trying to look so brave, as if she didn't care one jot that the horse wasn't hers any more. Without stopping to think, scarcely aware even that she was about to speak, Emma mumbled, "Nugget's a good name."

"What did you say?"

"I said, Nugget's a good name. It reminds me of the gold rose nugget you carry in honor of your sister."

"Yes. I named her Nugget because it was Susan and her gold nugget that made the horse mine." Katherine reached out and touched Emma's hand, the one with the ring. "Thank you," she whispered.

"Nugget," Emma said, patting the horse's neck. Yes, she thought, it was a perfectly good name and with a meaning of its own.

Weeks passed, with Emma practicing almost every day until she could canter and gallop and finally mastered trotting. The date was set. Next Sunday, almost a full week away. "Why not this week?" Tall Joe wanted to know.

"I am not quite ready," Emma hedged. "A few more days of practice and I shall be ready for anything. According to Katherine at least."

With each day, Emma dreaded the encounter to come. In her mind the scene played out in two very different ways. In the one, Tall Joe admired her skill and praised both girls for having the courage and good sense to choose a man's saddle. In the other, the one she dreaded, Tall Joe told her that no daughter of his would ride in such an unseemly fashion and if she refused to ride sidesaddle then she may as well stay in Victoria for the rest of her life.

As it turned out, she need not have worried. Neither event took place. On Wednesday evening, Tall Joe invited both Emma and Edward to dinner at the house he rented with his cousin and gold-mining partner, Ned Turner. When dinner was finished and the four sat around the little wooden table, Tall Joe sipped his coffee, glanced at his cousin, and announced that they had good news.

"Ned here heard of some land in the Nicola River Valley east of Cook's Ferry. We're headed up to see it."

"That's just in time then," Emma said. "Katherine says I'm ready for anything now. When are we leaving?"

Tall Joe avoided Emma's eyes and glanced uneasily from Ned to Edward. "We go tomorrow morning on the early boat."

"Oh, but I can't leave so quickly! I have nothing packed and it wouldn't be fair to Mrs. Douglas. Why didn't you tell me sooner?"

"It's the three of us going, Emma," Tall Joe explained. "If we pre-empt the property, I'll come back to fetch you."

"Oh. I see. And I don't have a say in the matter?"

"We thought it best if you didn't come along until we are settled."

"We?"

"It's rough country, Emma." Ned spoke for the first time. "No place for a young girl."

"I see," she repeated, her voice cold as ice. She turned to Edward. "And you are in on this too?"

"Emma." Edward's blue eyes pleaded with her to understand. "It's for the best. We need to look over the acreage to be sure it will make good farmland."

She glanced from one face to the other. And suddenly they all looked the same, all of them turned against her as if there were something horribly wrong with her. "I see," she said a final time and pushed back her chair. "An' what I might want counts for nothing." She walked stiffly to the door, grabbed her cloak from the peg and disappeared into the night.

"Emma! Emma, wait, you don't understand!" called a voice, a man's voice, one of the three. She didn't know whose, or care either. For now they all sounded alike.

Emma held the news inside of her all that night and into the next day. Every time she thought of Tall Joe, she grew angry. She had been right all along; she never could trust him. And she didn't need him for a father. She could take care of her own-self. But as cross as she was at Tall Joe, her fury at Edward was even worse. How could he treat her this way? As if her opinion didn't matter one jot. Well, and she wouldn't be speaking to him again in her entire lifetime, and that's for certain-sure.

"Is something bothering you?" Mrs. Douglas asked.

Emma glanced across the kitchen table. She shook her head, too upset to speak.

Mrs. Douglas sipped her tea and waited. When it became clear Emma wasn't going to reply, she said only, "I'll need you to wash the kitchen floor and clean the stove before you go riding this afternoon."

"If I go," Emma said without thinking. But now that she'd said the words they made perfect sense to her. If she didn't want a father and would never speak to Edward again, she wouldn't be going off to British Columbia with them. And she wouldn't need a horse. She wouldn't need to see Katherine again either. Emma was surprised how empty that made her feel. Seemed like she would miss riding the horse and chatting with Katherine. What else did she have to look forward to? Washing a floor. Cleaning a stove. Helping prepare dinner for the family.

"Why wouldn't you go? Are you not feeling well?" Mrs. Douglas asked.

"I'm quite well, thank you." Emma got to her feet. "And I'll get right to washing the floor as soon as I'm done with the lunch dishes."

Later that afternoon, as she made her way to Beckley Farm, Emma was bursting to tell Katherine what happened and why she'd not be leaving Victoria after all. The first hint of doubt hit her the moment she stepped into the barn. Along with the scent of horse and hay came the fear that Katherine would not understand. She walked slowly through the barn to the paddock where Katherine waited with both horses ready to go.

"Oh good, you're here, Emma. It's such a beautiful day, shall we get started right away?"

Emma nodded and walked to the block where Nugget stood. Katherine took the lead on Princess and they walked the horses single file along the path without speaking again.

At the field, Emma stopped beside Katherine, who looked up at her from Princess. The old horse had perked up over the months of being exercised every day. Even so, she couldn't possibly keep up with Nugget. Emma felt bad looking down at Katherine, who never once complained. "Would you like to ride Nugget today?" she asked on impulse.

Katherine's face lit up. "I'd love to," she said, "just a couple of times around the field, then we must walk a bit. There's something I need to tell you. It's so exciting I can hardly wait!"

"There's something I need to tell you too," Emma said, and immediately wished she hadn't. She needed more time to think this through.

Twenty minutes later the girls walked their horses side by side around the field, Katherine on Princess and Emma again riding Nugget. "What is it you want to say?" Katherine asked.

"Me?" Confronted with the chance to speak, Emma couldn't find words to get started. "It's not so important, why don't you go first?"

"No really," Katherine insisted, "you seem worried about something. Please tell me."

Before Emma could answer, Nugget stopped right there on the spot. Princess, never one to miss out on a rest break, stopped beside her. Emma needed to tell Katherine now, that or look foolish. "All right then, here's the problem."

Katherine listened while Emma explained how Tall Joe and the others had conspired against her. A little smile crept across Katherine's face when Emma said how the men planned on going off to search for farmland, leaving her behind where she'd never have a chance to say what she liked or didn't like or which farm to buy or where. Katherine didn't interrupt once, only listened with that annoying little smile growing bigger.

Emma's anger surged, not at the men but at Katherine. *Look at her, sitting there grinning like this was all a great joke.* Emma's cheeks burned, a hard knot gathered beneath her ribs, pressing outward, making it impossible to think clearly. Why did she ever think to trust Katherine? The girl was no different from those three men and Emma should never have told her anything at all. *And when would she learn, foolish girl that she was? No good ever came of telling your problems to others.*

Emma's first impulse was to turn Nugget's head, tap her sides, and gallop away. But she had almost finished her story and so spat out the last sentence. As if Katherine would care. "And those three up and left this very morning and never gave me a chance to get ready and come along."

Katherine's smile turned into surprise. "They've left? Already? Today? Oh, and just when I had some perfectly wonderful news from Mr. Roberts. Emma, I've been bursting to tell you!" She put her hand to her forehead, "And I planned for us to discuss it with your father this Sunday when he came to watch you ride!"

"An' 'aven't you heard a word I said?" Emma snapped. "I thought you would be angry as me, the way those men took off without a hint of their plans until the last minute when I couldn't do a thing about it. And Edward! He was in on it and could have told me if he wanted. And now you too! I thought you would be on my side, but you only sit there smiling like you've gone daft and talking about some wonderful news of your own. There's no one in this world can be trusted."

"Oh, but Emma, I am on your side, you've got to believe me! Wait while I tell you." Katherine twisted in the saddle to pull some folded papers from the large pocket of her skirt. "This very day I got the letter I've been waiting for. It's from Mr. Roberts, the store owner I told you about in Yale, remember?" Katherine unfolded the paper. "Here, just read this and you'll understand." She held it out to Emma.

Emma stared at the letter, covered in scratchy ink marks. She couldn't raise her eyes. How could she tell

Katherine she never did learn to read?

Katherine waited for a long moment then pulled the letter back. "I'll read it out loud. The man's handwriting is difficult to follow."

Dear Miss Harris,

I hope this finds you well and that you are enjoying your schooling in Victoria.

Your letter arrived safely here in Jamaica and I must say I was happy to hear from you. My time here on the island has flown past far too quickly. I have been helping my brother run the plantation since my arrival.

Your friend, Miss Curtis, sounds to be a wonderful companion for you and it pleases me to know that you are not so lonely as you were on the farm.

As it turns out, your suggestion came at a most opportune time. I would like very much to remain in Jamaica and help manage my brother's plantation. Therefore, I had been hoping for a way to avoid returning to Yale in order to divest myself of my store and property. I hesitated to bring up the matter with your parents, knowing their financial situation.

Miss Harris, I shall let you in on a little secret. Not only do I enjoy the company of family here along with the plantation work, but I have met a most wonderful young woman. Once all is settled and I have the money from my holdings in British Columbia, I plan to ask for her hand in marriage.

At the same time as sitting down to write this letter to you, I have also written to your father to make arrangements. Of course you will receive this letter before his makes its way to Yale on the sternwheeler.

The only impediment, as you pointed out in your letter, is that your father will need to sell his farm in order to purchase my store, stock, and property.

Miss Harris, I am impressed that you have thought this through in advance. Your idea of transferring title of your land and buildings to Mr. Bentley and his cousin, Mr. Turner, fits perfectly with everyone's hopes. They will have their farm, in a good area, not too far from Victoria and with easy access to transport their products down the Fraser River.

Your parents will be happy to live in a town, where they will not feel so isolated. They will make a decent enough living as Yale grows with the completion of the Cariboo Wagon Road.

You, of course, will benefit by getting off the farm you dislike so. I suspect too, with Miss Curtis living close enough, the two of you will visit often.

In my letter to your father I suggest he arrange with Messrs. Bentley and Turner to view the

acreage and, if agreeable, sign the appropriate
forms. Any improvements made to the property
will add greatly to its value.

All that remains now is for you to speak with the
gentlemen and advise them of the transaction so
they can arrange to meet with your father.

Yours sincerely,

Charles Roberts

Emma rested her hands on the saddlehorn, her fingers twisted around the reins. From that whole entire letter, one word stood out. *Friend.* Katherine was her friend. She was Katherine's friend. Emma had never had a real friend before, or been one either. The idea pleased her and frightened her at the same time, so she put it aside to think about later.

As soon as she did, something else began to worry at her. "You never said one word about Tall Joe buying your father's farm."

"No. I didn't want to get your hopes up, Emma. Or mine. I was afraid Mr. Roberts wouldn't like my idea. He does though, and I know my parents will be pleased too, once they receive his letter."

"The arrangement would have been perfect," Emma conceded, "if only his letter had arrived in time."

"Maybe it's not too late."

"'Course it is. When they come back, those three will have picked out their land, who knows where?"

Katherine folded the letter and slid it back into her pocket. "Then we have no choice but to catch up with them."

15

Catch up to 'em? An' how do yer s'pose we do such a thing, I'd like to know? I'm thinkin' I was right all along. Yer completely daft, an' that's for certain-sure!" Emma slapped a hand over her mouth. Her face turned bright pink.

Katherine gaped at her. Of course she had noticed the odd word slip into Emma's language here and there, but this time Emma's careful speech had fallen away completely. Poor Emma, she looked so embarrassed. In an effort to lighten the mood, Katherine laughed. "Not completely daft," she said, "even if my parents often think so."

But Emma refused to smile. She flicked the reins and walked away on Nugget.

"Listen, Emma," Katherine said, pushing Princess to catch up. "I've done it before. I went after George when he was off on his big adventure and we needed him at home. This time it will be easier, with two of us."

"You travelled up there, through that wild country all on your own?" Emma's dark eyes danced with suspicion.

Katherine looked away from those eyes that saw too much. "Yes," she said. "Mostly, partly on my own..."

The eyes narrowed. "And what did you say about friends telling each other the truth?"

"Quite right, but..." Katherine firmly believed that the only way to keep a secret safe was never to confide it in anyone. On the other hand, right now Emma needed to know she trusted her. "If I tell you, you must promise never to tell anyone, and most especially not my father, about William's part in it."

"I swear never to tell another living soul as long as I live."

"All right then, here's what happened."

They walked the two horses side by side while Katherine related her story. "It was my fault Father got attacked by an angry mother bear," Katherine began. "He was badly mauled and unable even to get out of bed, much less help Mother and me prepare for winter on the farm. There was so much to do that we needed George to come home and help out. He had left only two days earlier. I knew my parents would never let me go after him, so one night I borrowed some old clothes of my brother's and, dressed as a boy, sneaked out of our cabin..."

She told Emma the entire story. How she knew William was close by because he had passed through their property that very afternoon. She had tracked him down and asked for his help, since he knew the country so well. William didn't want to at first – he said she would slow him down – but he finally agreed to act as her guide through the Fraser Canyon.

"When we got to his village on the Thompson River, everything went wrong. William's father refused to speak to me. He stayed in the background, glaring at the two of us. With his father watching, William changed from being my friend. He acted as if he was ashamed to be seen with me and said I should go away. He said a girl can't be friends with a man." Katherine felt again the bitter tears she had shed that day. She blinked hard to make them go away.

"What did you do?"

"What else could I do? I got back on Nugget and left the village to search for my brother."

"Just like that? Weren't you angry?"

Katherine urged Princess into a trot and Emma followed suit, trotting Nugget alongside. Katherine spoke more quickly now, her words matching Princess' gait. "At first I was furious at both of them. But after a while I realized it wasn't William's fault. Or his father's either. William said his father is afraid of settlers. He sees us put up fences and claim the land for ourselves. He worries we will take all their land away. He believes there will be no more fish in the rivers. No deer in the forests."

"Well, but it seems like there's land enough for everyone in these new colonies."

"I think so too. British Columbia is four times the size of Great Britain and most of it empty land."

"Katherine, weren't you frightened, out in that wild country all alone?"

"Dreadfully," Katherine admitted. "But I had Nugget for company. And being dressed as a boy helped too."

"An' I should have done that when I ran off to escape that dreadful bailiff an' the workhouse."

"What do you mean?"

Just then, Nugget raised her head and waved it side to side. "Nugget needs a run," Emma said, and galloped off.

Emma didn't want to think about those frightful days after her mother died. She couldn't tell Katherine how terrified she had been, trekking across the countryside, seeking shelter, wearing old shoes of her mother's that never did fit right.

Racing around the field at full gallop, with the wind in her face, Emma tried to think. But thinking was difficult when you were flying across a field perched on the back of a great, huge horse. Even if she might be liking this horseback riding more than she ever thought possible, that didn't stop her from being scared every minute she rode at such breakneck speed. But she could not run away forever. Emma slowed to a canter and finally to a walk, waiting for Princess and Katherine to catch up.

"What was that about?" Katherine demanded. "I asked you a question and you ran off as if you'd been slapped. Please tell me, Emma, what's this about a workhouse? I read about them in *Oliver Twist*, and Charles Dickens made them sound perfectly dreadful, but I don't think they could be half as bad as he makes out. No one is so cruel as those people in his book."

"Well, and I don't know who this Oliver Twist is or Charles Dickens either, but my mother said in the workhouse they treat you worse than an animal, with never enough food and no heat and they make you work all day long for your keep. Mama said the workhouse was worse than any nethersken, and if you don't know, a nethersken is somethin' 'orrible!"

Memories of the tiny room she and her mother had shared took her by surprise. She smelled the foul smells and felt again the aching hunger in her belly. She shivered, recalling the damp cold that never went away all winter long. She saw her mother, lying on the hard floor, not strong enough to sit up for a sip of tea. Her throat tightened. She had never talked about her life in Manchester, not to anyone. How could she start now?

"Please tell me about it, Emma."

Nugget stopped on her own, as if she wanted to listen too. Princess took her cue and stopped beside the bigger horse.

Emma opened her mouth. Slapped it shut. A part of her wanted to tell Katherine, but something held her back. Some vague fear she didn't understand but was as powerful as her earlier fear of Nugget. "I can't." She studied Nugget's two ears, pressed back as if the horse knew what they were talking about and didn't approve.

"Of course you can, Emma, whatever it is." The saddle creaked as Katherine leaned forward to better see Emma's face. "Don't you trust me?"

Emma swallowed hard. Of course she trusted Katherine. Really she did. But still the words refused to form themselves. "It's only that I can't imagine how to begin."

"All right, then. Why not tell me about your escape from a bailiff? Why was he after you? And what's a nethersken?"

Well, and the girl doesn't know about netherskens – always being rich and pampered as she was and giving no thought to a poor girl without shoes on her feet and not a scrap of food to make her mother well.

"Emma?"

"A nethersken's where me an' me mam lived," Emma snapped. "Not like you, growin' up in some fancy toffken, lookin' down on poor folk with no place to live but on the street."

She heard Katherine's quick intake of breath. When she looked, Katherine was gazing off toward the trees. If the girl had gotten angry, that would be one thing. Emma knew how to answer anger. But she had hurt Katherine's feelings and that was something else, something Emma had no idea how to fix.

"I'm sorry I don't know about netherskens," Katherine said. "And I guess you want me to be sorry for where I grew up. But I don't understand why you get so cross. Tell me, Emma, did you have a choice about who your parents were or where you were born?"

"Of course not. How could I?"

"You couldn't, yet you seem to believe I did. Emma, my parents were never rich, even if we did have enough food every day and a comfortable enough home we shared with my grandparents. They all worked for what we had. If my father had been content with that life we would still be in London and my sister would still be alive. But Father always wanted more. He insisted Susan and I get an education and learn to ride horses in the event we might someday meet upper-class gentlemen who would deign to marry us.

"Father envied the landed gentry and yearned for land of his own so he could pretend to be one of them. That's why we packed up and moved here. But Emma, where I grew up, I never once saw children living on the streets or knew anything about workhouses or netherskens, either. If that makes you angry, I'm sorry, but I can't change anything about it."

Emma's anger ebbed away with Katherine's words. "I get so cross sometimes I can't control what I say," she admitted. "Words come flying from my mouth and I don't

DAYLE CAMPBELL GAETZ

know how to stop them." She started Nugget at a walk, and Princess kept pace. "Ladies like that Mrs. Morris who think themselves better'n a girl who arrived here on a brideship make me so angry I want to scream. But I know you're not like them, Katherine. And your mother's kinder too, and that's for certain-sure."

"My mother's trying her best. And the truth is my father used to be a terrible snob, but even he's getting better. He feels so guilty for bringing us here. Nothing is what he thought it would be."

"For me, everything is better than it was in England," Emma said.

"Please tell me." Katherine waited, but when Emma didn't reply, she suggested, "Why not begin with the nethersken?"

"All right then." Emma took a moment to gather her thoughts. "In winter we had no heat but a cooking pit in the cellar, and coal smoke crept into all the grimy little rooms above. People were jammed ten and more to a room, and the only water was what we collected from a pump two blocks away."

"And that was better than the workhouse?"

"The workhouse is for those who have no job and no place to live. People who run workhouses make sure they are worse than any nethersken for fear every worker will up and quit to go live a life of ease in the workhouse." Emma fidgeted with the reins, wrapping them tight around her fingers. "From the time I was small, we worked in a spinning mill, me mam an'...uh, my mother and I. That's how we could afford such luxuries as a cold an' bare little room to ourselves with tea, stale bread, and potatoes for food."

She unwrapped Nugget's reins from the fingers of one hand, wrapped them around her other hand. "But then a war started over in the United States, an' all those poor slaves who picked the cotton stopped working. With no more cotton being shipped, we had no jobs. My mother took sick, and I tried to take care of her, but she died anyway and there was nothing I could do about it."

"Oh, Emma..."

Emma held up her hand. Once started, she didn't want to stop until she was done, the words spilling over one another she spoke so fast. "Before she died, me mam made me promise never to set foot in a workhouse. But he came for me the very next day, the bailiff did, and grabbed me by the arm. He said it was for my own good." She rubbed her arm, picturing that horrid little man with his fat belly and those nasty little eyes that looked her up and down and made her feel sick to her stomach. "An' he called me a cripple."

Emma gulped back tears. "But I'm not so crippled as other children, crawlin' under those machines from the time they're no more 'an five, cleanin' out dust all day long, keepin' the machines runnin', squeezin' into spaces so small their bones never did grow right. An' when they grew up and couldn't walk, they were sent off to a workhouse or left on the street to take care of their own-selves."

Emma became aware that both horses had stopped walking once more. She had no idea how long they had been standing this way with her going on about herself.

"I'm so sorry, Emma. I had no idea..."

"An' it's not your fault for not knowing," Emma snapped. She hoped Katherine understood it wasn't her she was angry at. She took a quick breath and slowed her words. "I ran away and that horrid bailiff was too old and fat to catch me. So I kept on walking, right out of Manchester to the countryside my mother always said was so beautiful but I had never once seen."

She told Katherine how frightened she had been, travelling at night, hiding during the days. At last, cold, half-starved and exhausted, she found her way to the door of a parsonage, and the parson's wife, Mrs. Barnes, took her in. "I thought Mrs. Barnes liked me and if I worked hard would let me stay. But come summer she sent me off on the *Tynemouth* with sixty young girls, mostly orphans plucked from the streets and workhouses. They stuffed us in the hold like cargo and kept us there. Even when the steamship arrived at Esquimalt Harbour, they never would let us out for three more days."

Her words sped up again, remembering. "An' they lined us up an' marched us like cattle through the streets with all those disgusting men gawkin' and shoutin' vulgar things." Emma felt her face flush with the anger and humiliation of that day.

"And that's when I first saw Edward." She sat up straighter in the saddle. "He was the only one decent enough to look embarrassed at the men's behavior. Edward smiled at me and made me feel less ashamed."

"Emma, it's those men who should be ashamed, not you."

Emma couldn't think how to answer. Anger churned inside her like a wild beast she could not control. "We should take a run before dark," she said, and took off at a gallop.

Darkness crept around them as the two girls walked their horses toward the barn. Katherine removed Nugget's saddle and turned to face Emma. "Which way do the men intend on going?"

"Is there more than one way?"

"They could catch a boat to Yale and head through the canyon. Or they might travel by sternwheeler up Harrison Lake to Port Douglas and from there by several boats and trails to Lillooet. It depends on where they plan on looking for land."

Emma tried to think. "I only remember Tall Joe talking about a river. It has a pretty name and it's after you cross over the Fraser River on some ferry."

"Cook's Ferry?"

"Yes. That's it! And I remember now, there's land Ned Turner heard tell of on the Nicola River."

"That's good then, because I expect they'll stop at the general store in Yale for horses and supplies. We'll need to leave tonight and be on the steamer first thing in the morning."

"This very night? But how can I tell Mrs. Douglas I'm running off? If Governor Douglas hears of it, he'll never let us on that steamer. He's a strict man who doesn't believe any young unmarried girls should go off travelling on their own."

"Don't worry, Emma, because you won't be on your own, and neither of us will be a young, unmarried girl."

"Wot? An' have you gone daft? What can we be but unmarried girls? And those men at the dock won't let us on the boat. They'll send for Governor Douglas to take us back home, an' that's for certain-sure."

"All right then, Emma, you must promise not to tell anyone, not even Mrs. Douglas. Once you tell a secret even to one person, you lose all control of it."

"But Mrs. Douglas is so good to me, an' she'll worry if I up and leave."

"Then I'll write you a note to put on your bed."

Emma hesitated. Did Katherine realize she could never write such a note on her own? "If you help me, I can write it my own-self. My mother schooled me some when there was time and we weren't too tired."

"Good then, that's what we'll do."

But Emma still felt bad. "Mrs. Douglas needs my help."

"Can't she manage on her own for a time? From all I've heard, she is quite capable."

Emma considered. "She is. And young Martha has been learning how to help out too."

"Then I'm sure they'll get by for a few days."

"Maybe. But how do we get ourselves on that boat?" Emma asked.

"I have an idea. Tell me what you think."

16

Emma rose in the chill black of early morning. She felt her way through solid darkness down the stairs and into the kitchen, where she felt safe enough to light a candle. She stoked up the fire in the woodstove and set about preparing porridge for the Douglas family's breakfast. Just as she placed it to simmer on a back burner, there came a quiet tap on the back door. She scurried to open it. A dark figure slipped inside.

Emma stepped back in surprise. Outlined against flickering candlelight was the clear outline of a man's wide-brimmed hat, and below the hat a jacket and long trousers.

A hand flew up, whipped off the hat, and plunked it on Emma, where it settled over her forehead. The same hand pushed it back to sit more comfortably. "We will make a man of you yet, my son." Katherine giggled.

"But is that really you, Katherine?" Emma whispered. "I would never have known it."

"Splendid, because isn't that our plan?" She bowed from the waist. "And now, if you will allow me to introduce myself, my name is Albert Jones."

"Pleased to make your acquaintance, Albert." Emma curtseyed.

Emma led Katherine up the dark staircase to her attic

room. Once inside with the door shut tight, she lit a candle and turned around for a better look at this Albert Jones. In her man's shirt, vest and jacket, and those trousers that hung down over her boots, Katherine could easily pass as a boy.

"You've cut your hair again!" Emma remarked. "An' it was already short for a girl."

. "I had to, Emma, it was getting too long to pass as a boy." She picked up the hand mirror from Emma's dresser and gazed into it. Her straight brown hair lay against her neck at the back and stopped slightly below her ears at the sides. "I think it suits me just fine, don't you?"

"You look like a boy, but wearing clothes too big for him."

Katherine took off her jacket. Removing her little cloth bag from the pocket, she wrapped her fingers around it. "Which is why you will wear George's old clothes. They'll fit you better than me. I only wore them here to avoid being noticed by men leaving the saloons. Did you find an outfit for me?"

Emma gave her a neatly folded pile of clothing. "These are clothes young James hasn't worn for some time, as he's growing so fast. The breeches are knee length, but by the look of them they'll fit you well enough. There's a shirt and wool jacket. There's even a cap."

The girls changed quickly into their new clothing. "You'll never look the part of a young man with those two long braids trailing beneath your hat," Katherine said. "Sit down while I cut your hair."

Emma picked up the mirror. She swung her head side to side, watching her braids fly out, catching the candlelight. "Couldn't I simply pin it up under my hat?"

Katherine shook her head. "That's what I thought, but

William insisted on cutting it and I'm grateful he did, or I would have been found out more than once."

Emma couldn't look while Katherine snipped her hair away. But as soon as she finished, Emma picked up the mirror. The face looking back was so much like Tall Joe that she slammed the mirror down. "Joey Bentley at your service," she sighed.

"Not quite," Katherine said. "Just look at your hand."

Emma gazed down at her ring. She touched her fingertips to it. Slowly, she pulled it from her finger. "I used to wear it on a string around my neck so no one would see."

"That's too risky," Katherine said.

"But I can't simply stuff it in my pocket, what if it got lost?"

Katherine pressed her lips together, thinking. "All right then." Slowly, she pulled the little cloth bag from a pocket in her new breeches. "Let's slip your mother's ring in here with Susan's nugget, and we'll leave them both in a bureau drawer until we return."

Halos of misty light encircled every gas lamp as the two made their way through town. Emma shivered in her new clothing. Katherine pulled the wool cap low over her forehead.

Men milled about the docks, but none gave a moment's notice to a couple of young men who kept their distance. When it came time, the taller one purchased tickets for his young friend and himself.

"We've done it, Joey," Katherine whispered, as the steamship pulled away from the dock. "We will switch to a sternwheeler in New Westminster and by tonight we should reach the farm. Won't George be surprised?"

Emma shifted uneasily on the seat. Why should she

care what George thought, one way or another? She had never met Katherine's brother. But Tall Joe, there was another matter. The man would be shocked to see her, and that's for certain-sure. And he might decide he didn't want a daughter after all, not one who behaved in such unseemly fashion. And if he tossed her out of his life, Emma wondered, how would that feel?

Not so good. Not good at all. *And what are you doing here, you foolish girl? Setting yourself up for disappointment, that's what. Looking forward to living on that farm and having a father to care about you? With a friend who lived not so far away to visit now and then? Riding a horse and exploring the countryside when there's time to spare?*

No good ever came of looking forward to things that never would come true. And no good ever came of letting yourself care about another person. She should have stayed where she was, as a housemaid for Mrs. Douglas. She was safe enough there.

"What's wrong?" Katherine asked.

Oh. Emma realized she had made an odd little sound in her throat and now couldn't think how to answer. Katherine would never understand this fear deep in her belly, this dread that if you got your hopes up, they would come crashing down around you.

"Because if you're hungry, I can fix that." Katherine opened her bag and pulled out a neatly wrapped package. She handed Emma a thick slice of bread with butter and jam.

"Thank you." Emma bit into it, relieved she wouldn't need to explain. "Thank you, this tastes good."

After a long day's travel, the girls disembarked and walked along Hope's main road, guided by lamplight that spilled from windows and lanterns held high by townspeople who milled about, greeting other passengers. Katherine watched Emma looking around as she walked, her huge eyes taking in everything. She poked Emma in the ribs with an elbow.

"Why did you do that?"

"You have got to look more a man of the world," Katherine whispered, "not some young girl gawking at everything she sees. And Joey, don't take those dainty little steps of yours, as if your legs are confined in a long skirt. William showed me how to walk like a boy, with long strides and your head held high. He said to hold your arms out from your body and turn your elbows out. Watch me."

Katherine walked ahead, exaggerating the length of each stride, pressing her shoulders back, trying to look bigger than she really was. She held her arms at her sides, elbows bent as if about to draw a gun from a holster.

Emma stood tall, changed the position of her arms, and took a long stride. On the next step, her weight landed on her right leg and she toppled forward. Catching herself, Emma adjusted her stride until she walked with a noticeable limp but took longer steps than usual. In this way they followed the road out of town under an almost full moon and a sky brilliant with stars.

"Is your leg hurting badly?" Katherine asked.

"It's not so bad. And there's nothing to be done about it."

"But are you certain of that, Emma? Have you seen a doctor?"

"I don't need a doctor to tell me my bones never did grow right, crawling under machines from the time I was small," Emma said. "I'm far from the only one, and my leg isn't so bad compared to most."

Here was something else she never knew, Katherine realized. English children forced to work until their very bones became deformed. One day she would ask more about it, but since Emma's leg seemed such a sensitive topic, Katherine decided instead to inquire about Tall Joe. "Emma, I know it makes you cross to talk about it, but I still don't understand why Tall Joe left you behind where you and your mother suffered so. He seems like a decent enough man who wants to be a father to you."

"An' he's a bit late, don't you think? My mother died because of him."

"Then why do you want anything to do with him?"

"I didn't at first, I was that angry. Growing up, my mother told me he died of the typhus."

"Why would she do that?"

"Seems like Tall Joe and my mother loved each other, but he had so little money her father refused to let them marry. The man was a country parson who had big ideas of bettering himself."

"Like my father?"

"No, not so much, not by buying land for himself. The parson wanted my mother to marry an old man who owned land and a fine house."

"What happened?"

"My mother refused. Then Tall Joe heard about gold being discovered in California and next thing you know he and Ned Turner up and left. Just as they've done to me now."

"And he never wrote?"

"Those two men didn't do so well in California. And

even if he did write, it was too late. My mother found I was on the way and went to her father for help, but that man kicked her out of his house and never spoke to her again. That's how she ended up dying a pauper."

"Oh, Emma, how dreadful. I can't imagine a father being so cruel, even if your mother did make a huge mistake."

"But, Katherine, aren't you afraid of your own father learning about your friendship with William?"

"That's different. Father would be angry and I wouldn't like that, especially if he took it out on William. But my father loves me and would never kick me out of his house no matter what. Anyway, with a little help from me, he would get over his grumpy mood soon enough."

Emma limped along for several yards. "Then your father is a more reasonable man than Tall Joe, who has his own set ideas of how a girl should conduct herself. And I'm not so sure I can behave well enough to keep him happy."

"Emma, if that's what's worrying you, I can help. You see, I've had a father all my life and have learned how to handle them. Fathers need to be taught how to behave. They don't know it on their own. They think they must get cross if you don't do things their way. They don't understand you can think for yourself and do what's right all on your own, so you need to show them. My sister understood that and tried to tell me, but I wouldn't listen. It was only after Susan died that I figured it out for myself."

"Figured what out?"

"That getting angry doesn't work, not on fathers or anyone else."

"Well an' that's not so easy then," Emma said. "Sometimes anger grows so big inside me I can't do anything but let it out on whoever's near."

DAYLE CAMPBELL GAETZ

"An' seems like I've noticed that, Emma. Seems like I have." Oh! She had done it now. Katherine hadn't meant to make fun of Emma or copy her way of speaking. She had only meant to lighten Emma's mood. But those words had spilled out of her now and she couldn't get them back.

Emma's head whipped around.

Katherine winced. She searched for words to make things better. None came to her.

"An' if gettin' angry won't work on you," Emma said, "I may as well try somethin' else."

"May as well." Katherine laughed. She sighed then and shifted her bag from one arm to the other. It seemed heavier with every step.

"There's something I don't understand about laughter," Emma said, "since I never did it much before. Isn't laughing supposed to make you feel better?"

"Of course. A good laugh can turn bad times into good."

"Then why does it sometimes make you sad?"

Oh. Katherine stopped, put down her bag. "It's because of Susan. We used to laugh so much together."

Emma stopped too. "And that's what your sister would want? For her memory to make you sad?"

"No, of course not. Susan would want me to be happy. It's only that, so often when I laugh, I think of her."

"And you feel guilty for being the one to live."

Katherine didn't reply. She didn't need to. It was enough that Emma understood. She picked up her bag and the two trudged on in silence.

"There it is," Katherine said some time later.

"I don't see anything."

The cabin was no more than a square of solid black against a dark background of forest. Not the faintest glimmer of light showed in the windows. If it had not been for a whiff of woodsmoke clinging to the still air, Katherine would have thought no one was home.

"The cabin is there all right," Katherine assured her. "It will be warm inside and there'll be hot tea and something to eat."

They crossed the distance with renewed energy.

Katherine stopped at the door, uncertain whether to knock or walk right in. She didn't want to take George by surprise in the dark of night. No telling what he might do. So she rapped as hard as she could with her knuckles, the sound muffled by the solid wood door. There was no answer.

"What if no one's here?" Emma whispered.

"George is here all right. He's likely asleep. He gets up early and works hard these days."

She pushed open the door and stepped into a pitch-black room, dragging Emma behind her.

"Who's there?" a voice bellowed. Heavy footsteps tromped from the room their parents usually slept in. A lantern burst into life and was thrust in Katherine's face.

After a moment of shocked silence. "Oh my Lord, what next?"

The light swung away and was thrust toward Emma, who backed toward the door.

"And exactly who would this be? Katherine, don't tell me you've run away with some young man?"

"Um, George, I'd like you to meet my good friend, Joey," Katherine said. She turned to Emma. "Don't worry, this is only my brother, George. He's perfectly harmless – for the most part."

"What in God's name are you doing here, Katherine?

And dressed like a schoolboy? Father will be furious when he hears of this."

"If you'll only calm down, George, I'll explain everything. But first my friend and I really need to sit and rest. This has been a very tiring day." She guided Emma to Father's chair at the table and then settled herself on one of the less comfortable seats. "A cup of tea would be lovely," she added, "and a bite to eat."

George plunked the lantern on the table and glared from Katherine to Emma and back again. "He's wearing my clothes." He jerked his head in Emma's direction.

"Yes," Katherine agreed. "And they fit better than they did on me."

George stepped closer, removed the hat from Emma's head and bent to stare into her face. "Is he a girl?"

"An' wot if I am?" Emma snatched back her hat and replaced it on her head.

"Listen, George," Katherine said wearily, "we're tired and hungry and we've come all this way to help you get off this farm, just as you want. So if you'll only bring us some food before we faint dead away from hunger, we'll explain everything."

George straightened up. "Off this wretched farm?"

"Yes." She gazed longingly toward the kitchen.

George hesitated for a moment longer, then picked up the lantern and padded to the kitchen in stocking feet. The girls were left in semi-darkness, although the cooking area was mere steps away.

"Is your friend William here too?" Emma whispered.

"I hope so, because we need the both of them. But I can't say he's my friend, because that's not what he wants. He and George are friends now though, having worked together over the winter."

George returned with tea, bread and butter, and a plate of dried venison. Katherine and Emma ate hungrily. George looked from one to the other. "Are you going to tell me what you're doing here?"

Katherine took one more bite of bread, chewed, and swallowed it with a gulp of tea. She put her cup down. "All right then, George, this is what's happened."

With Emma jumping in every so often to clarify, add details, or insert her own point of view, Katherine explained what had brought them here.

"And you want me to go after the men?" George asked when they were done.

"If you think that, you don't know your own sister very well," said a familiar voice behind them.

Katherine whipped around. And there stood William, blending with the shadows beyond the lantern's glow. His arms were folded across his chest, and he leaned against the doorway to the back bedroom. She wondered how long he had been standing there.

He nodded in her direction. Katherine dipped her head in response. Of course they couldn't be friends, she understood that now. William would soon return home and marry that young woman he talked of. Her own life would head in an entirely different direction.

"William's right," she said to her brother. "I don't need you to do anything but loan us Duke for a few days."

When George didn't reply, she added, "Also a pair of your trousers, if you don't mind, long ones that I can tuck into my boots. These breeches are too short, as you can see."

George grunted.

Emma shot him a puzzled look.

"Don't worry," Katherine told her. "My brother only grunts because he can't think what to say. He might sound scary, but as I say, he's perfectly harmless, aren't you, George?"

She laughed when George grunted again.

William grabbed a cup and joined them at the table, pouring tea for himself. "You will need to borrow Coal also. George and I will have both horses ready for you at daybreak."

"Thank you, William." No, she thought, they couldn't be close friends, that was too much to expect, but they could always help each other where needed.

Finally George spoke. "I can't let you go running off into the wilderness on your own."

"Why not?" Katherine asked. "I've done it before and you know it. Besides, I won't be alone, because Emma will be with me."

"Father would never forgive me."

"If you're afraid of Father, then I suggest you don't tell him. If it comes to that, I'll say we borrowed the horses when you and William were off working and didn't know a thing about it."

While her brother sat there scowling, Katherine took a moment to make proper introductions.

"William, this is my good friend, Emma Curtis. Remember, I told you about her last time we met? For now though, we're calling her Joey. And Joey, I'd like you to meet my – uh – a friend of our family, William."

They all set about eating until not a scrap of food was left on the table. Katherine stood up to clear the dishes. "I'll clean up in the morning," she said. "And pack some food for our journey. Right now, I need some sleep."

17

There's the store." Katherine hunched low in the saddle. "Stay close beside me as a shield in the event one of my parents comes out."

They kept the horses close together, Emma on Duke and Katherine riding Coal. Katherine turned away from the row of wood-frame buildings to her left and gazed down the low bank at the wide river flowing past on her right side. She heard men's voices and imagined them seated on chairs beneath an overhang, puffing on pipes and trying to outdo one another with their stories. If Father was among them, all was lost.

"Keep on at this same pace so we don't call attention to ourselves," Katherine whispered. But Coal chose this moment to raise his head, pull on the reins, and prance sideways along Yale's narrow dirt road, pulling well ahead of Duke.

"You there, on the black horse!" A too-familiar voice called from her left.

For a half-second, Katherine considered ignoring the voice and galloping out of town as fast as possible, but knew this would only call attention to herself and Emma. She pulled Coal to a stop. Her heart raced.

Mother stood on the wooden sidewalk, one hand

on a half-open door. Her eyes moved from Katherine to Emma. She closed the door and marched onto the dusty street, directly to Coal. She reached up and grabbed his bridle. "What on Earth are you doing here, Katherine? And who is this?" She gasped in surprise. "Not Emma?"

"I'm sorry Mother, but something's happened and we need to catch up with Emma's father."

"But...I don't understand. Isn't he in Victoria?"

Emma spoke up then. "Tall Joe and his cousin, with Edward to help them, have run off to choose land on their own."

"We need to catch up before it's too late," Katherine added.

"Oh dear. And only this morning your father and I received a letter from Mr. Roberts. I have our reply ready to mail." She raised her hand, holding two letters.

The men's voices grew suddenly louder.

Mother's fingers tightened around the bridle. "Katherine, your father will be joining that group at any minute now. He can't fail to recognize the horses."

She was right. Her father would recognize Duke and Coal in an instant. What did that matter though, when Mother had already stopped them? "The men have come this way, Mother, we're sure of it. If we catch them in time, I know they'll be interested in buying our farm over pre-empting a vast tract of uncleared land."

Mother tapped the letters against her forehead. "Katherine, it must have been them who stopped by the store only this morning. Those three can't have gone far with all the supplies they purchased. They've taken horses and a pack mule, which will slow them down." She gazed up at Katherine as if deciding what to do.

"Will you let us go then? Please?" Katherine pleaded.

A burst of laughter erupted from the men behind them.

"Take this." Mother handed one of the letters up to Katherine.

"Thank you, Mother." Katherine tucked the letter into her pocket. "You won't be sorry."

"Be safe." Mother let go of Coal and stepped out of the way.

Katherine and Emma rode out of town side by side, wanting to gallop, keeping to a walk. Once out of Yale, they moved slightly faster, but the trail was rough and didn't allow for a gallop.

"Aren't you going to read the letter?" Emma asked.

"Not now. If we hurry and are very lucky, we might catch up with them before nightfall."

They rode on, single file, with the sound of the river in their ears. Mile after mile they travelled until the sun sank below the treed hills and the temperature began to drop.

"Seems like it will soon be dark," Emma complained. "And this looks like a good place to stop or are you planning to ride all night?"

"We'll stop soon, Emma. If I remember correctly, there's a flat place to camp not far ahead. We won't want to tackle the canyon in the dark."

"An' what's this about a canyon?"

"A rocky trail too narrow for one horse to pass another. Sheer rock walls straight down to a narrow gorge where the river rages through. More than one horse has been lost over the edge."

Gathering darkness forced them to stop with no sign of the men. Katherine started a campfire, and the girls huddled close to it for warmth, with black night all

DAYLE CAMPBELL GAETZ

around them and a million stars overhead. They made tea and ate the bread and dried venison Katherine brought.

Katherine pulled out Mother's letter and read it by firelight.

"Well then? What does it say?" Emma asked.

"Oh, at first some stuff about how they miss me. But here's the interesting part. My parents are excited about Mr. Roberts' proposal to sell them his store and have already replied to his letter. Look, Emma, they've enclosed a letter addressed to Mr. Joseph Bentley and Mr. Ned Turner." Katherine held it up. "Mother says it explains all the details and terms of purchasing the farm. They want me to deliver it." Katherine folded the letter and tucked it away. "And that's exactly what we're going to do, you and I."

"We are indeed," Emma agreed. "Exactly as your parents asked."

"We'll start again at first light and hope to catch them before noon."

"And before this canyon of yours." Emma shuddered. "It sounds like somethin' 'orrible!"

Katherine laughed. "You'll be fine, Emma, if it comes to that. You're a good horsewoman now."

"Thank you," Emma said. "You're a good teacher." She stared into the fire. "Katherine? Do you think I could ever learn to read and write?"

"Of course you can, Emma. All you need is a good teacher." She laughed. "And I happen to know there is one available."

Emma smiled her thanks.

The campfire slowly died, but Emma lay awake, gazing up at the stars, worrying what tomorrow might bring. She yawned and closed her eyes, drifting into a dream-filled sleep.

She looked down. Straight down to a narrow cut between steep-sided rocks. Tons of water funneled through with a roar that echoed up the canyon walls. She clung tight to the saddlehorn. Pressed both knees against Duke's sides. Ears forward, the white horse picked his way over loose rocks on a trail that narrowed with every step.

"You're no daughter of mine!" Tall Joe yelled, so close his warm breath spilled over her cheek. "I want nothing more to do with you!"

Startled, Emma lurched sideways. Duke lost his balance, tried to recover, but stepped too close to the edge. Loose rocks gave way, bouncing and crashing down the rock face. Horse and rider followed.

"Aihhh!" Emma screamed, but the sound stuck in her throat. Her body jerked.

"Are you all right?" Katherine asked.

Emma opened her eyes. By firelight, she saw Katherine add another log to a crackling blaze. Steam rose from a blackened pot. Emma tried but couldn't speak. Her chest hurt. She had forgotten to breathe. The dream refused to let go.

Katherine poked the fire with a stick, scattering bright orange sparks into the night. "What were you dreaming that made you moan like that?"

"I made a real sound?" Emma asked, sitting up, blinking.

Katherine nodded. "As if you were being strangled in your sleep." She handed Emma a mug of tea. "Here, drink this, it will help you wake up."

"Already? But it's still dark night." Emma shivered. "And cold enough for frostbite."

"The sun will be up soon. We need to get an early start." Katherine poured herself some tea and sat down on a rock. "What were you dreaming about, Emma?"

"Tall Joe." Emma could still see the anger on his face. His words still rang in her ears.

"That's what frightened you?" Katherine handed her a slice of bread.

Emma bit into it, thinking what to say. "That an' tumblin' to my death in the canyon. I'm thinkin' Tall Joe will be that angry at seeing us. Maybe I should have stayed in Victoria, where I belong."

Katherine, about to sip her tea, lowered the mug. "Emma, if you say so we can still turn back. It's not too late. That would be the safe thing to do. Perhaps you don't mind carving a farm out of the wilderness with no cabin to live in and no fields ready for planting come spring. And only those three men for company because it will be too far for us ever to visit."

"But Katherine, I have another choice. I don't have to go with them at all. I can stay in Victoria and take care of myself."

"And I can return to living on the farm," Katherine said, as if she didn't care one way or another. But she turned away, blinking hard.

"Is farm life so terrible then?" Emma asked.

"No. Not for the right people." Katherine gazed into the fire. "If Susan had lived, I might even have liked it. But my teacher, Mr. Brett, tells me I have a talent for teaching, Emma, and it's something I really want to try.

As it happens, there are a lot of youngsters up in Yale who need schooling."

"But what if it doesn't work out? What then?"

"I don't know, Emma. At least I will have tried." She bent to place a small log on the fire. "Is that it, Emma, are you afraid of trying something new?"

"I'm not afraid..." Emma began, but couldn't think what else to say.

"Or is it Tall Joe you're so frightened of? Are you afraid if you let yourself care about him he might hurt you one day?"

"No. I'm not..." Emma stopped to think. Is that why she felt so frightened inside? Because she feared Tall Joe wouldn't like her so much if he got to know her better? Maybe. And if she turned around now, she might never know. "Could be it's the dream that's frightened me and nothing more. Let's go catch those men before it's too late. And whatever happens, we'll have done our best."

"Good then." Katherine jumped to her feet. "By the time we have the horses ready, it should be light enough to see where we're going."

Around each bend, Emma hoped to see them. She listened for voices up ahead, the snort of a horse, anything. But all she heard was the roar of the Fraser River far below. The land fell away so sharply it seemed they walked on the edge of the world. We must be nearing the canyon, she thought, and still no sign of the men. Her dream was about to come true. "Katherine!" she cried out, but Coal had outpaced Duke, putting Katherine too far ahead to hear. Emma was glad of that because, really, she had nothing to say. Only that she was afraid.

"Hurry along now, Duke," she said, "or we'll be left behind."

DAYLE CAMPBELL GAETZ

Duke walked faster, but Coal picked up his pace as well. Neck outstretched, the black horse sniffed the air and lengthened his stride. Katherine and Coal disappeared around a bend.

Duke followed at a slower pace. The trail widened. A small stream tumbled down a narrow crevasse. Horses and a mule were drinking from the stream, where it pooled beneath the rock cliff. A young man tended to them, his back to her. Edward?

Duke stopped just short of bumping into Coal.

Emma became vaguely aware of men's voices, a cough, the contented snort of a horse. The acrid smell of smoke. Bacon cooking. She turned toward the campfire. Stopped breathing.

Tall Joe stood up, clutching a frying pan. "Hey there fellows!" He waved a greeting. "You're welcome to share our fire. We'll be on our way in no time."

Emma's voice lodged itself at the back of her throat.

"We'd be grateful to join you," Katherine answered. "And we have food of our own."

At the sound of her voice, Edward turned, his eyes wide and staring.

"You're a young lad to be out on your own." This was Ned speaking, on the far side of the fire. He added another chunk of wood.

Tall Joe placed the frying pan on a rock and started toward the newcomers. "Your voice is very familiar," he said, his eyes never leaving Katherine's face.

"I wonder how that is," Katherine said. She swung down from the saddle and turned to look up at the tall man who had closed the gap between them.

"Your face is familiar too," he said, scratching his

beard, "but I can't seem to place it."

Katherine removed her hat. "Albert Jones at your service." She gave a deep bow, flourishing her hat.

Emma remained on Duke, ready to turn and flee at any second. Edward left the horses and moved closer to the newcomers. She glanced at him, and he smiled as if happy to see her. She looked away.

"But...you're not...you can't be...Miss Harris?" Tall Joe looked Katherine up and down, his face hard. "What is the meaning of this?"

Without giving Katherine time to reply, he pushed her aside and strode over to Emma. "Emma?" He glared up at her. "You've followed us? Dressed as a boy? And riding astride a horse! Have you no shame, girl?"

Oh, and here it comes now, Emma thought. *He will send me away and never want to see me again as long as I live.*

But Tall Joe wheeled around on Katherine. "I hold you accountable, Miss Harris. You must have put Emma up to this. She never would have done such a thing on her own."

"It was both of us, Tall Joe," Emma said, careful to keep her voice calm in spite of a knot of anger that wedged itself beneath her ribs. "Katherine has some news to share, and if you had only waited one more day instead of running off, you could have saved us all a lot of trouble."

If Tall Joe heard her, he gave no sign. "This country is no place for two young ladies on their own. How you made it this far without meeting disaster I'll never know."

"And yet we are here," Emma pointed out. She took a deep breath to calm herself. "Not only that, but we started a day later and caught up with you."

"It's unfitting..." he stammered. "Young ladies should never..."

In spite of Emma's efforts, the knot inside her grew out of control. "Oh, an' I suppose it's fittin' to run off and leave me alone, same as you did me mam?"

Tall Joe's face collapsed.

Emma glared down at him. And she didn't feel sorry, not a bit of it. She spoke the truth and it needed to be said. And more besides.

Katherine cleared her throat. Looking up at Emma, she pressed a finger to her lips, shaking her head ever so slightly. Emma took the hint and let her friend take over.

"Mr. Bentley," Katherine said, "Emma and I have an important matter to discuss with you. It involves an excellent opportunity to purchase a farm with a good-sized cabin, a barn, and a well already in place, with much of the land already cleared. There is even a milk cow included in the sale. I call her Genevieve."

Emma rolled her eyes.

"Rather than pre-empting acreage way out there in the wilderness," Katherine said with a sweep of her arm, "you could have a comfortable home to live in and crops planted this very spring, with easy transport down the Fraser to markets at Victoria and beyond."

While Katherine talked, Emma dismounted. She stood at Duke's head, the reins held loosely in her hand. The anger was still there, but she forced it down, forced herself to speak in a calm voice, like Katherine. "At least listen to what we have to say, Tall Joe," she said, surprised at the way her anger shrank with every word. "We've come all this way to tell you."

"I can't believe you would do this to me, Emma. What

were you thinking?"

"I did nothing to you, Tall Joe, except try to stop you from making a second mistake. Where's the harm?"

"You could have gotten lost," he sputtered. "Or been killed!"

"But I wasn't, as you can see. And we have good news to share, if you'll only listen. Katherine, why don't you show my father the letter?"

Tall Joe stared at her. His beard split in a smile. He blinked as if there was smoke in his eyes.

What happened?

Tall Joe strode over and wrapped her in his arms. Emma didn't pull back, she didn't even mind. It was then she realized what had changed between them. For the first time ever, she had called him her father. And it didn't feel half bad.

"An' don't go gettin' all mushy on me, Tall Joe," she said, pulling away. "Shall we all sit by the fire and discuss our plans?"

Tall Joe read the letter and handed it to his cousin.

When Edward was reading it, Tall Joe said, "I don't suppose it will hurt to take a look at this farm."

"It sounds the perfect set up," Ned Turner replied, puffing on his pipe. "At my age, I'm ready to choose a degree of comfort and a farm closer to civilization."

"We'd be closer to Victoria so I can visit my mother and the children," Edward added.

"Good then. Hurry and eat up those bacon and beans you have cooking," Katherine said. "We've a long way to travel back to Yale."

"An' seems like we'll need to go real slow so's you men can keep up," Emma added.

DAYLE CAMPBELL GAETZ

Tall Joe, reaching for the frying pan, stopped and glanced up sharply. Ned Turner leaned forward, puffing black smoke from his pipe. Edward put down the letter, removed his hat and ran his fingers through his hair.

Emma's cheeks grew warm. Her words were meant to tease, but not one of them looked to be laughing. Well, and she had a lot to learn about joking. And families. Friends too.

Then Katherine broke the silence. "We can try, Emma," she laughed. "But going so slow won't be easy, and that's for certain-sure."

Author's Note

Taking the Reins grew quite naturally out of two historical novels I wrote several years ago.

The first, *The Golden Rose*, tells Katherine's story. In 1862, fourteen-year-old Katherine travels from England to British Columbia with her family. Both Katherine and her sister, Susan, are excited about this big adventure. But once on their land, reality sets in. Susan dies of "Panama Fever," and the bereaved family attempts to carve a successful farm out of this rugged and untamed new colony. A task that proves too much to bear.

The second novel, *Living Freight*, is Emma's story. After her mother dies as a pauper in Manchester, Emma is determined to keep her promise and never let the authorities place her in a workhouse. So Emma sets out on foot for the English countryside and eventually finds herself on the bride ship, *Tynemouth*, headed for the colony of Vancouver Island.

Taking the Reins answers a question many readers have asked over the years. "What happens next?" I have to admit, I've often wondered the same thing myself. And that got me to asking, "What if?"

For those of you who wonder where ideas come from, my answer is simple. For me, most stories begin with those two little words, What if...?

About the Author

Dayle Gaetz is the author of more than twenty books for young readers, including the YA novels *Spoiled Rotten*, *Crossbow* and *No Problem* and two mystery series published by Orca Book Publishers.

She began her writing career on Salt Spring Island, where, alongside publishing sixteen novels, she wrote a column for the local weekly newspaper and articles in children's magazines.

Dayle's books have been shortlisted for several Young Readers' Choice Award programs, including the OLA Silver Birch Award, the Red Cedar, and MYRCA, as well as for the Geoffrey Bilson Award for Historical Fiction.

She lives, writes and teaches in Campbell River, BC.